The Amphibiots

ISBN: 978-1-63950-043-7   [Paperback Edition]
        978-1-63950-044-4   [eBook Edition]

Printed and bound in The United States of America.

Writers Apex

Gateway Towards Success

8063 MADISON AVE #1252
Indianapolis, IN 46227
+13176596889
www.writersapex.com

THE AMPHIBIOTS

CLEMENT S. MASLOFF

Chapter I

anid Rolius had a horrific dream the night before his hiring interview at the Archivum. He was a child once again, and the victim of an Anuran street gang. Half a dozen large, muscular bullies with large orange armbands chased him through the early morning fog as he fled to the safety of the district Salamandrine school. Stones hurled from slings zipped past his head. One of them finally felled him onto the hard beton of the street, leaving him with a stinging head wound. As the attackers approached the injured student, the siren of a patroller wagon began to sound ever louder. The ruffians scattered as two adults jumped in and came to the rescue of the nearly unconscious boy.

The pair questioned him about the incident. He had better go home and miss school for the day, one of his defenders advised. No, protested the victim. He must show enough strength to continue and not surrender to violence. The adults helped him to his feet. Ranid still suffered torturous pain. He felt his head, then looked at the blood on his hand. The Salamandrine patrollers offered to accompany him to school. The youngster heroically replied that he was well enough to walk the rest of the way there. That afternoon he was supposed to play in a game of shinny, and was obligated to be present.

Ranid awoke in a cold sweat. He glanced at the illuminated time-ticker on his bedstead. The memory of what had happened to him over twenty years before grew dim. His mind concentrated upon the scheduled interview with the Praeposter of the Salamandrine Archivum. Every hope of his years of study depended on winning the research position he was applying for. Ranid leaped out of bed and began preparing himself for what lay ahead that day.

Throughout the land of Caecilia, religious zealots of the two opposed denominations were familiar with the name of Hyle Xalus, a rising star within Salamandrism. He had started as a humble predicant in a poor country parish, then was assigned to a slum oratorium in the capital. His rising reputation as an eloquent sermonic lector brought him to the attention of the hierarchy in his sect. This resulted in promotions to large, important congregations. His outstanding talent in preaching the doctrines of the Salamander led to a teaching professorship in the School of Predicants, where he aspired to becoming the Head Rector one day. But the career of Hyle took an unexpected, unforeseen turn when, out of the blue, the Salamandrine syndics placed him in charge of the archival library of their organization. A high post, indeed, but not the one that for years he had dreamed of occupying.

Hyle now doubted that he would ever climb to the Concilium of Syndics and exercise the highest power within the hierarchical structure. He had to be satisfied with being the headman of records and manuscripts, nothing more than that. After several years of supervising the Archivum, his low spirits and ennui became permanent, it appeared to him. What had he to look forward to? the Praeposter asked himself once again on the morning that Ranid Rolius came to see him about the job.

The young man who appeared exactly on time was unusually short and thin. His skin had a fulvous sheen, more yellowish than gray. Bright hesperidic eyes glowed with inner energy. As the two shook hands, the taller Hyle Xalus smiled warmly at the candidate. Ranid sat down and studied the older man for a moment.

Large and stocky, the Praeposter possessed taupe-colored skin of a darker gray than that of Ranid.

Xalus began the interview with a direct, abrupt question.

"Why do you wish to take this research position, brother?"

His hepatic eyes, dark and bloody, stared keenly at the surprised scholar.

Ranid leaned forward in his lockwood chair.

     CLEMENT S. MASLOFF

"I want to delve back to the time, a hundred and seventy years ago, when the Amphibiots divided into the separate denominations that exist today. How exactly was it that the original unity dissolved so completely? The general outline is known to all of us, but there are important questions that remain enveloped in mystery. These are not abstract, academic matters. I believe that the archival sources can strengthen our Salamandrine claim to priority in time. We existed first, and it was the Anurans who broke off in schism from us. It was our Institutor, the immortal Alsike, who discovered the true path of enlightenment. Our ancestors were the genuine, orthodox believers. It was the frog-worshipping Anurans who dissented and revolted, straying from the true track, which is ours."

For a short time, Hyle Xalus made no reply, startled at the fervor of the candidate for employment. When he spoke at last, his voice was much slower and lower than before.

"What you say is extremely interesting to me. There can be no doubt that any research into the founding era is fraught with consequences for the faith we hold. It would be useful to us if your work could firmly, finally establish the proof of our historical priority. We would then have a powerful weapon against our enemies."

"That is my foremost hope, sir," asserted Ranid with determination.

"What would be your specific area of investigation, may I ask?"

"I plan to search all the papers of our founder, Alsike Caldus. How did he come to the concept of odyle energy within a particular amphibian species, as we recognize it in the Salamander? My goal will be to trace the process by which the Founder reached his conclusions. How did he create the system that we Salamandists adhere to today? That is what I want to clarify.

"I intend to show how straight was the road he took, remaining the True Amphibiot from start to finish."

The Praeposter considered the situation for only a few seconds.

"Yes, you are the man we need for this vacancy. The project you described is exactly what can serve us in our conflict with the foe. I believe that your work here should start immediately, brother."

He rose, gesturing to the overwhelmed Ranid to follow him. They went to the large repositorium where the records of the Salamandrine organization were stored.

Chapter II

Ranid made brief notations of salient statements he found in the personal writings of the great Alsike Caldus.

It was curious to him how little was known about the intimate life of the Institutor, thought the scholar in moments of reverie. He left behind more about his private, inner meditations than his personal life, that much was clear after long, arduous study of the primary sources. There were mysterious empty spaces in his biography.

Diary entries by the Institutor recorded deep revulsion at the state of spirituality in his own age. The concept of the odyle had become an abstract, distant force beyond human perception or understanding. Who any longer could grasp the idea of the infinite, the unbound? The odyle was now understood as unknown, invisible, and ineffable. No wonder only a small handful of believers ever thought about or considered such a difficult spiritual subject. It seemed very distant back in that age.

On the other hand, noted Alsike, popular tradition was rich in folklore that dwelt on the supernatural attributes of different amphibians in Caecilia. Unlettered sages predicted fortune and misfortune based on signs from such creatures. Amphibia occupied an important area in the minds of the mass of people, noticed the Founder. This was so in no other country anywhere, only in his own native land.

Alsike was, therefore, aware of both the spiritual and folklore factors involved in all thought. He wrestled with the task of combining the two strains, though they appeared so different. They belonged together in human thought about the supernatural, it would seem.

Ranid focused on key passages of the manuscripts written by the great man long ago.

- The odyle that moves all the universe must have central modes, from which the planes of all being originate. Our predecessors have failed to identify these within our own world. It is only in these modes that the celestial ecliptic can be found, yet all have failed to uncover them. They have remained mostly unknown and invisible.

- The task of our age is to identify a particular being as the main node.

- I am investigating amphibians with what I term my odylic instruments. The work goes on without visible end. But the point I hunt for will, in time, be pinned down. Of that I am certain.

- It has become necessary for me to leave the capital for the countryside. There may be a better chance of narrowing the hunt for nodal centrality outside the cities and towns of this land. My expedition will take me through areas where there are large populations of amphibians of all kinds. Is one of them the medial agentive of the odyle? Can one species provide the solution that I seek?

There was a silent gap of three weeks after that in the diary and notes of Caldus, discovered Ranid. Why was that so? What had caused it? Had something unmentioned occurred?

When the Founder returned home to the capital from the countryside, he wrote nothing about what he had done or seen on his trip. His mood seemed one of deep disappointment to those who saw and met him. He had made no progress in his search. His work had to start all over again, as if nothing had been found out in the countryside.

But Ranid asked himself whether Alsike had misjudged what was happening to him. Within less than a year, Salamanderism was created and wholly constructed. How did that happen so quickly? he wondered. The journey about Caecilia had long been ignored, minimized, and overlooked by scholars. But was that an error? Had this key to everything been obscured by earlier scholars?

CLEMENT S. MASLOFF

The new investigator decided to examine the journey period in full detail. But how was he to begin? Where was he to start? There would be enormous problems involved without written sources.

All at once, a novel idea struck him. Local collections of Salamandrine documents might contain reminiscences of the persons Alsike visited and spoke with. That might be a source from which to learn about this obscure period of time. It could contain important secrets never considered before, he suspected.

Ranid consulted with the documental librarians of the Archivum.

Yes, they informed him, the regional archives were brought here decades before. Only rarely did anyone look into them. They lay on the shelves unused, gathering dust.

I must dive into them at once, the young researcher said to himself.

Ranid examined records and notes from various regions and different localities. The work was long and tedious. But one morning he grew excited. His search for new, unstudied material led him to a seaside village named Calluella and a naturalist signed Bufe Ascaphus. His eyes poured over this man's handwritten words with growing curiosity and fascination.

- Yesterday a stranger arrived from the capital, a scholar traveling with faradaic field apparati and many notebooks. I conversed with him at length. What are you looking for? I inquired. What he told me was most interesting and enticing. He believes that there is one particular species of amphibian that holds spiritual primacy over all the others, in fact over all of nature. This being is the only true intermediary representing the odyle in this world of ours. This single variety of amphibian is the key to enlightenment and salvation. But what is its name? I demanded to know of him. He was unable to tell me, for that name remained unknown to him too. That is why he took to traveling, in order to find that out. That is what this man was after. What particular amphibian would unlock all metaphysical secrets for him?

- At first I laughed at this odd-sounding fellow. But there was something so genuine and sincere in his manner that my view of him swiftly grew favorable. He was no fool or fantasist. The man truly believed in his quest. Gradually, I started to become fond of him and decided that I would try to help him to the degree that was possible.

- One day, in his rented flat overlooking the Inland Sea, I asked him what I could do to assist. His answer astounded me. The center of his attention had become the proteus, a type of amphibian I myself was unfamiliar with. We both looked up and studied what had been written about this rare, unusual creature. It was of absorbing interest for both of us.

- Blind, water-breathing, with a tail, the proteus lives in limestone caves along the coast, most often beneath sea level. Small and resembling the eel, it possesses four tiny limbs and a narrow head. There are three toes on each of the anterior legs. The snout is oddly flat and truncated. Hidden beneath its face skin are very minute vestigial eyes. The flesh is a pale green. There are two plane-like external gills that are blood red. The proteus has always been considered uncommonly rare, a freakish inhabitant of coastal caves. Why this enraptured interest on his part? I dared ask the young scholar that question. It holds the key, was his answer. Enlightenment can come out of it, he told me in close, strict confidence. The man asked me to help him with his faradaic detectors that he was going to use on a proteus, the longest-living of all Amphibians.

- This morning the sky was clear, the weather mild and pleasant. The two of us set off early, carrying the instruments in a donkey-pulled cart. I took my friend to a deserted shore area where I was certain there were many caves. Both of us dove into the quiet waters. He was the one to locate the first proteus, probing it with a detecting rod. This took at least a quarter of an hour. He looked me in the face with despair in his eyes and said that the test had failed. The man was very disappointed. There had been no success at all for him.

   CLEMENT S. MASLOFF

- He tried out three more captured protean amphibians that day. All of them showed nothing of spiritual significance on the faradaic dials. I have never witnessed such disappointment. His heart was crushed. What he had hoped to find was not there. What had gone wrong? he asked me. In silence, the two of us returned to my cottage in Calluella.

- Though I tried mightily, it was impossible to cheer up the scholar. What way out was there for him? I suggested that he take a new, different direction from what he was already doing. His ears seemed to perk up as he listened to me. I remember how he sat at my small ironwood table where we ate our meals together. What did I mean? my friend asked me. What sort of innovation did I intend to recommend?

- It came to me in an instant flash. I proposed an answer to him. The salamander, further evolved than the proteus, became the suddenly conceived solution he was hunting for. We have a rich variety of amphibians along the coast. The one that is spiritually gifted must be somewhere there. The one being sought is probably unsuspected. He became eager to begin testing of the new creatures. With energy and enthusiasm, the man studied the simplest of salamanders, the newt and the eft, the triton and the triturus. He appeared to be inspired with a new energy and ambition.

- In the morning, I was exhausted from a sleepless night of worry. Had I done wrong in giving him a new interest and an enthusiasm for exploration? I could not go out on the water with him to hunt for salamanders. He had to take a boat out without me along. Stay in bed and rest, my friend ordered me. The time passed slowly that day. Most of that morning and afternoon I spent in sporadic slumber. I felt sick and restless. He returned very late, entering my cottage quietly, so as not to disturb or awaken me as I rested.

- I was surprised upon becoming conscious to hear him say that he intended to leave in a few days. Why was that? I asked. Had something gone wrong? But no explanation came from the spiritual searcher. Few additional words were exchanged between the two of us. My guest refused to tell me anything about what had happened that day out on the water. Only much later did I surmise that he had made a discovery of faradaic sensitivity in some species of salamander. He left without informing me what precisely it was he had found.

CLEMENT S. MASLOFF

Chapter III

Ranid decided he had to go to Calluella and hunt for confirmation of what the document implied about the Institutor at the time of his spiritual breakthrough. Had the great man first concentrated his attention on the proteus, as the local man said he did? New questions arose in the mind of the young researcher and they drove him into travel to the decisive spot.

"I need a short vacation," he told the Praeposter of the Archivum. Not a word was dropped about the precise goal of his plan for a trip. Only when he had what he was after would he make any revelation of what he had been up to.

A magneto-train took him to a depot near the coast. Then a local mule-drawn charabanc carried him to Calluella. Arriving near dusk, Ranid went at once to the village inn and rented a room. From the second-storey window, he had a panoramic view of the bay and the harbor beyond the ancient fishing community, bathed in blue summer light.

He gazed down with awe at the dories, dinghies, and fishing smacks tied up at a wharf. A few of the craft might qualify as piscine sloops or schooners. Others were poor, simple cockleboats or gondolas. He had read in geographic guidebooks that the local population went out on the Inland Sea to catch bream, bass, scup, hogfish, pilchard, shad, and herring. A few connoiseurs brought back porgy, cuttle, trigger, balloon, filefish, globefish, and puffers. The rarest and most valued of the sea game were the sparoids and asteroidals that could be sold at high prices in towns and cities. Many were exported to other lands as well.

The young visitor went to bed early, soon after night fell. The journey had tired him. Tomorrow he would search for possible links to the past and the origins of the Amphibian system of belief.

Hungry felids meowed along the pier in the dawn light. Brilliant yellow rays lit up the harbor and the sea. Most of the fishing boats had already left when Ranid set off to locate the village tax office.

A clerk helped him look up the records that he wanted to see. Yes, there was a family with the name Ascaphus now living in Calluella, on the outskirts near the shoreline. The woman gave him the address and directions how to find the dwelling. It was surprisingly easy to locate the small cottage. On the low chimney of the stucco structure stood the green symbol of a frog. It was plain what that meant. The Ascaphus family belonged to the Anuran faith and revered one particular amphibian, the frog. In some regions these believers called themselves Batrachians, in others they were Salientians. But wherever they lived and whatever their label, they were all frog-oriented Anurans.

Some members of this Anuran sect centered their attention upon Bufonidic toads, while others looked to tree frogs or bullfrogs for inspiration. The Grylio and Catesbian were prominent frogs in some places, as well.

Ranid rapped at the xyloid door until a white-haired, short, and stubby man appeared.

"Is this the Ascaphus home?" inquired the stranger from the capital. "If so, I have some important business with the senior member of the family."

"Come in," said the householder, leading Ranid into a tiny, cluttered parlor. The two men sat down facing each other on plainwood stools.

"I am Ichno Ascaphus. No one in the family has my age or seniority. My days of fishing, however, have been over for a number of years. How can I help you, sir?"

Ranid cleared his throat, then presented an imaginary explanation of his business and presence in the village. "I am writing a work about old families of historical importance. Your ancestors are of great interest to me. I noticed that this dwelling displays the Anuran insignia. That is fascinating.

　　　　　CLEMENT S. MASLOFF

Do you have any recollection of how your forefathers came to follow and believe in that faith?"

The other drew a deep breath. He was formulating words and phrases for his reply.

"My paternal grandfather explained it as a result of an unhappy incident far back in the past. Let me try to remember his description of how it happened. There was an early Ascaphus in our direct birth line whose first name was Bufe. He experienced an unhappy confrontation with an early Salamandrite here in our village. I was never told the specific cause of this quarrel. But the result was that Bufe Ascaphus refused all attempts to convert him to that type of worship and belief. He was completely opposed to all their teachings concerning the salamanders. The way my grandfather explained it to me, there was a sort of feud between our ancestor and one of the important pioneers of that heresy. The split arose from this personal clash with a leading light of that stream of thought.

"Bufe Ascaphus turned down all attempts to convert him to that other sect. I am no philosopher and do not understand all aspects of the conflict. But this division remains a central core of family history for us down to today. All the sons and daughters of Bufe became Anurans as soon as that faith was brought and preached here. And their descendants have never strayed from belief in the frog.

"Is that what you wished to ask me about, sir?"

Ranid searched for the words he needed.

"I have heard that it was the famous Alsike Caldus who visited here at that time. Do you think that he could have been the man who quarreled with your ancestor?"

The old fisherman wrinkled his brow as he searched his memory.

"That could be so, but it was so long ago. Who can be perfectly certain after so much time has passed? But I have often told myself it could have been the person you mentioned just now. Yes, he could have been the individual involved in the dispute."

Ranid unexpectedly sprang to his feet. "Thank you for your assistance. I must be going now. But I am in your debt for what you have revealed to me about what occurred here so many years ago. It has been a great help to me."

"I know only the little that has been passed on to me," groaned the oldster. "My own sons have heard the story, but no one can know whether they too will retell it to their children. We will have to wait and see. That remains in the future."

Ranid shook hands with Ichno, then made a speedy exit from the small cottage.

There had been no need to reveal the specifics of the diary notes of Bufe Ascaphus that he had discovered at the Archivum. It did not mention any Anurans in this village, only the Salamandrites. So the scholar explained and justified to himself his silence on that subject.

He had come there to listen, not to speak or expound anything on his own.

As the magneto-train clanged along its rails back to the capital, Ranid tried to sort out the implications of all he had learned in his private probing.

The Institutor had first attempted to advance a new doctrine centered on the proteus. But an obscure local naturalist had opposed him on this so strongly as to shake the mind of Alsike Caldus to its foundations. It was at the suggestion of this Bufe Ascaphus that the Founder had moved on to new spiritual possibilities, settling upon an unforeseeable faith that was created in the mind of Alsike after and because of this outside suggestion, the proposal from Bufe Ascaphus.

Everyone knew today that he had reached the conclusion that the perfect salamander with spiritual supremacy was the axolotl. It had been upon that particular species that the new movement of the Founder was established.

Had it been Bufe Ascaphus who had proposed such a solution to him? Was he the unknown, unseen factor in the beginning of modern Salamandrism?

     CLEMENT S. MASLOFF

But why, then, had Bufe argued so angrily with Alsike Caldus? Why had he turned to Anuranism, away from the Salamandrine faith?

Deeply perplexed, Ranid groped for a way to explain the complex birth of the spiritual sect to which he himself belonged.

The night aboard the magneto-train was a sleepless one for the lonely young traveler. He arrived back in Caecilia City in the first light of dawn, tired and sleepy. He was thoroughly confused over what course to take next.

He concluded that he had to seek advice and guidance from Hyle Xalus, Praeposter of the Archivum. His consul must be asked at this point. What will he think of all that I uncovered on my expedition into the past of the Institutor? Will he see value in the topic that I am studying?

What becomes of my findings will be in his hands.

Chapter IV

For Alsike Caldus, the axolotl had become the genuine acme, the apex of spirituality in every sense.

Ranid reviewed and reread what Salamandrine scriptural texts said about that particular amphibian.

"The axolotl is the living symbol of the sacredness of the salamander. It represents and stands for all salamanders, large or small, wherever they may dwell. Whether spotted or black, mottled or single-colored, the axolotl is the highest form of living being. Once hunted down as a delicacy, it must today be protected from harm by the force of law. It alone possesses the attribute of neoteny, whereby its reproduction occurs as early as the larval stage. No other amphibian has anything similar to the larval reproduction of the axolotl.

"As an adult, the axolotl lacks the typical gills found in amphibians, but has to depend upon its special lungs. This makes the axolotl a unique, unmatched salamander, the summit of all spirituality. There is nothing like it in the whole of nature."

Sitting in his study cell through the night, Ranid wracked his brain for a solution.

How was it that Alsike hit upon the axolotl as the epitome of the amphibian spiritual essence? Official histories of Salamanderism saw the origin of this core idea as a lightning flash of inspiration during the Founder's mysterious journey to the sea coast. But what was the reality of that trip? What had actually occurred there that had led to the birth of their sect?

     CLEMENT S. MASLOFF

He still lacked an adequate answer to these questions, Ranid told himself. Perhaps more reading in the local collections of documents might put him on the right road to an answer.

The researcher decided to explore beyond the notes of Bufe Ascaphus. Were there other persons who met and influenced Alsike Caldus when he visited Calluella at that crucial turning point in his life? That was a possibility worth exploring.

It did not take Ranid long to locate what he was after. The diary notes of a Brag Omphalus, a local notary, revealed a second factor, overlooked by everyone. There was an influence on the Institutor even greater than that of Bufe Ascaphus.

The young Salamandrite was shaken by this second revelation found in the Archivum. He read on with pulsing heart, learning what had been buried and forgotten.

- The invisible odyle must have its emissaries and interceders in this visible world. As far back as time goes, this question of intermediacy lies at the crux of all spirituality. Who is the agental being that represents the infinite and sublime?

- Who can be the sacred intercessor for human beings? In the watery land of Caecilia, it has to be an amphibian animal, no other kind will do.

- The odyle of the universe is difficult to comprehend. What can stand for it yet remain a particular, substantive being? Someone must know that. It was the ancients who once had that knowledge and can tell us if we study what they said back then.

- Old people, in scattered moments, speak of the lizards of earlier times. These were the sacred apods. Did our ancestors know and recognize them? Why have we of the present age forgotten what they once were?

- Today a stranger arrived here from Caecilia City. He claimed to be investigating traditional folk spirituality, but I have grave suspicion of him. He associated for a time with a local naturalist and made excursions on the water with him, but then the two of them broke up and quarreled. No one knows why. The stranger insisted upon speaking with me, because he heard that I am familiar with the ways of old. This young scholar was open and candid, I found. He is hunting for a sacred amphibian. I told him to look into the past and find out what was once known about apods. I promised him that he would experience a startling surprise if he did so.

- The stranger asked me to introduce him to our special cryptic circle. What was I to do? The other members, at first, were suspicious of him and refused to let him enter among us. I argued in his behalf, convincing them that he posed no danger at all. So, for several weeks this man attended our apod circle. He rarely said anything, except to ask questions. I could sense that he was absorbing the lore concerning the apodic lizards that we love and worship.

- I learned that the outsider has left Calluella overnight. Someone said that he had more trouble with the local naturalist, but I know nothing of that.

Ranid took time to ponder and think out the meaning of what he had unearthed in the inner recesses of the archival collections. His brain was fundamentally shaken, his mind unhinged.

His native land was called by the ancient name of Caecilia, derived from the appellation for legless lizards. These were the earliest, most primitive amphibians. They were the evolutionary ancestors of all future species that were to appear later. No amphibian was older in terms of time.

Apodal caecilians had always squirmed over the ground here. Did earlier humans worship them? Possibly. Were they also the earliest emblem of the odyle? Had ancient temples been built to them? Were they the center of original spiritual enlightenment?

There was nothing in either folklore or history to contradict that suspicion.

　　　CLEMENT S. MASLOFF

An even more important matter was the position of Alsike Caldus toward the circle of Apodists he had come into contact with in Calluella. Had he absorbed any of their ideas? What was the actual influence on him of this early sect? Did he become one of their members?

Ranid decided to make an appointment to see the Praeposter at once.

The implications of what he had uncovered were astounding ones. If the Institutor and Originator had once belonged to this Apod circle in Calluella, that surprising fact changed the entire accepted, standard history of the formation of the Salamandrine system of belief. It also transformed all the credenda of the Anurans as well. Everything in spiritual life stood in danger of being overturned.

Ranid was compelled to acknowledge that what he had found out was genuinely revolutionary. Was he to suppress what he now knew to be true? Should he bury or destroy the evidence he had come upon?

Only the Praeposter could help him out of the dilemma he faced.

Hyle Xalus appeared to be astounded by the scripta on his desk. He read them over several times before looking up at the young man.

"What does all this imply, Ranid? Are we to conclude that a quarrel with Ascaphus pushed the Institutor away from a focus on the proteus and that a secret apodic circle then recruited him for a short while? These supposed findings of yours threaten to stir much commotion in our Salamandrine spheres. They would certainly turn our understanding of our history upside down. There would be general confusion among our masses of believers. They would have to deal with total confusion concerning how their system of thought arose.

"I foresee the potential for enormous conflict should the Anurans get hold of those two sources that you found. Their predicants would rage night and day against our claim to priority and originality. They would surely call us schismatics descended from earlier, primitive Apodism. There could be widespread unrest, even violence if that should happen, I am afraid.

"Who can predict or foresee the results of publicizing your discoveries?

"I can see general confusion and disruption among our followers, let alone the officiants and ministrants of our faith. Shock and panic would infect all ranks of Salamandrism.

"Both you and I need experience-based advice, Ranid."

"Who can provide us that?" inquired the latter.

Hyle thought a moment. "The Capitular of the Syndics, our highest official. He alone will know what to do about the matters you have uncovered."

The Praeposter promised to make arrangements to see the man at once.

Ranid left in a quandary. What had he begun? The supreme prelate of his sect was now about to look at his findings. What would be the reaction of that authority to these surprising discoveries in the Archivum? How would he deal with Ranid and his surprising research?

Chapter V

Claudo Eximius was the most senior and powerful magistral in the Salamander Organization. No other syndic was near him in stature or personal authority.

The tall, gaunt skeleton moved slowly with deliberation as if existing on a different level from others. His eyes had an eerie sherry color, his short hair was a clean snowy white. Everything about him was distinctive and impressive. It was obvious that he considered himself magnificent and important.

What kind of emergency can there be in the Archivum? the elderly official asked himself as he made his way to the magnificent office he occupied as the Capitular of the Salamandrine faith. The message from the Praeposter had requested this meeting to take care of some urgent problem at the Archivum. What sort of trouble could be expected to arise among the stacks and piles of scripta? wondered Eximius.

A long career within the Organization's hierarchy had taught him many hard lessons. Cruelty has its uses. In fact, it was in many situations a necessity. One had to know when to apply brutal harshness to a situation. He had learned to nurture pitilessness within himself. Yet ruthless violence was often over the line, mainly because it did not work. Excessive force could easily turn counterproductive, if it was carried too far. He had learned from experience that each case was different. But in general, a moderate, reasonable degree of pressure got things done in the high, important post that he occupied.

Hyle Xalus, with Ranid at his side, entered the great temple building made of agate, sand flint, and silica where the Salamandrine faith had its main executive offices. This mountain of a structure was called the Citadelle.

Hundreds of clericals worked at high, slanted xyloid desks. On the highest floor of the castellum was the office of the Capitular, to which the pair of visitors climbed by a spiral stairs of cast iron.

A famulus led them into the spacious sanctum of the supreme leader. They were told to sit down on soft fanteuils and were served cups of jequirity by this servant. Their wait continued, a sign of respect for the figure they had come to see.

Without fanfare or introduction, the old man slowly entered the chamber. As the Capitular approached them, Hyle and Ranid rose to their feet, placing their cups on a small tabular. "Please, be seated," said the syndic. He nodded to the famulus, who brought over an official cathedra for the high magistral to sit in, then left the room.

"What is it that you wish to see me about?" asked Caudo Eximius, staring directly at Hyle. The latter introduced Ranid, then described in detail his two discoveries. At first, he spoke slowly and hesitantly, but as he went on his statements grew firm and definite. Finally, the narrative by the Praeposter came to an end.

The Capitular studied Ranid for a time, then asked him a question.

"It is all as he describes?" His face had taken on a pinkish glow.

The researcher cleared his throat, then began in a quiet, uncertain tone.

"Yes, the contents of the two diaries are exactly as just presented. There can be no doubt about what the words written there mean. They speak for themselves."

"And what is their significance and spiritual meaning? Can you reveal that to me, young man? I doubt that is possible for anyone not versed in the science of hermeneutics. That is a special talent for interpretation that only long experience with sacred texts can bestow on one. I believe that neither one of you has acquired that capability. Since it will have to be used on these two diaries, let me think a moment so that I can provide a preliminary symbolic interpretation for the two of you."

 CLEMENT S. MASLOFF

The pair from the Archivum remained mum as the great magistral cogitated to himself. After several minutes of thought, the old man began to whisper in a low voice to them.

"The history of the Amphibiot faith in this land of ours was much different from what conventional books say about it. Long before the Great Schism between Salamandrites and Anurans there existed a certain very small particularistic sect that was centered upon the limbless lizards and apods. There is no trace of it in any official versions, but the group was there. Yet its role was a crucial one. It was the earliest specification of one species of amphibians as the messenger of the odylic power and energy. As these discoveries show, this tiny sect played an important part in the thinking of our Institutor. It was these Apodics who guided his early spiritual course."

Caudo Eximius said nothing as he looked back and forth between the two men. He seemed to be preparing himself to make a weighty statement, a spectacular clarification of the whole subject before them.

At last, he rose from his official chair and stepped closer, until he stood next to the two fauteuils.

"I cannot avoid telling you a private, concealed secret. Not a word of it can ever be exposed to anyone else. Is that understood?"

Both visitors affirmed that it was. Each promised to keep silent about what was to be revealed to them.

"You are now pledged to absolute secrecy," said the Capitular. "Never forget that."

He returned to the cathedra and seated himself again.

"We of the Salamandrian leadership have always possessed a secret knowledge meant only for a small number of chosen ones. The syndics who direct our organization share in this hidden matter. I myself, as Capitular, participate in this deep mystery. Every one of my predecessors in this office had knowledge of this concealed arcanum. It has been passed on down the generations, starting with our Institutor, who served as the Founder and Originator of our faith. I only bring this out before you today because of what this young scholar has now run across in the Archivum."

He looked intently at Ranid, then continued.

"You mentioned the diary of Breg Omphalus as well as that of Bufe Ascaphus. Neither of those two individuals has any place in our official history. Yet they were both forces that helped make our Founder what he became. They molded his thinking into the specific form it took. Between the two of them, they made our system what it now is: an outer shell and an inner core that differ profoundly between what they hold to be true.

"As was revealed in the diary of Bufe Ascaphus, our Originator found his link to the odyle while he was alone on the water off the coast. This evolved into his doctrine of the axolotl, the sacred salamander. He turned against his friend and mentor, keeping secret this event. Why was that? Why was a radical break with Bufe made necessary under these new circumstances?

"His faradaic instruments told him that the axolotl was the keystone, the conduit to the odyle. But at the same time, the notary named Breg Omphalus was able to convert him to a very old belief, that in the primitive apods.

"How was this dilemma solved in the thought and conscience of Alsike Caldus? How was the gap bridged between the one and the other, the salamander and the apod? How did our Founder make a consistent, integrated whole out of his binary mode of thought?"

The Capitular stopped to draw a long, deep breath. The two visitors gazed at him as if in hypnotized states. What was he getting at? What was the leading authority implying?

"Alsike remained, till the end of his days, a secret Apodic but a public Salamandrite. It was impossible for him to draw a mass following to the lowly lizards. That special faith was kept for the few chosen for high authority in our denomination. This configuration became solidified into permanency with the Great Schism. The war against Anuranism necessitated stricter secrecy. The inner kernel of Apodic belief had to be protected from exposure and attack. This conflict continues today. So does the secret dualism that can never be acknowledged. We are a mass faith that contains an arcane inner brotherhood. The many are directed by the few, of whom I am one. No

   CLEMENT S. MASLOFF

one beyond the high leadership knew this truth until you stumbled upon it within the bowels of the Archivum."

Absolute silence ensued, until Hyle Xalus spoke up.

"What will our future hold, now that this knowledge is also ours?"

Caudo Eximius gave as sympathetic a look as he could.

"The two of you will continue, of course, in your present posts. There must be consultation among the syndics. What I believe will happen is that both of you shall be invited to join the Apodic grouping at the center of our organization. That will entail initiation into the secret inner faith. You shall both become adepts in the hidden spirituality. That will take time. For the present, continue to work with patience at the Archivum. When everything is settled and decided, I myself will come to you and guide your progress. I can foresee organizational promotions in the future for both of you."

Suddenly he shot up out of his chair of high office and abruptly dismissed them. Neither visitor said anything to the other as they departed. They were both stunned and disoriented by the revelation just made before them.

Chapter VI

Ranid was appalled and disgusted with the hypocrisy exposed to himself and Hyle. How could such duplicity exist for so long a time? How was it that no one outside the conspiracy ever had the least suspicion? Falseness and duplicity rose to incredible dimensions within the framework of the system most precious and meaningful to both of them. They were both shaken by what they had been told.

For several days, Ranid lived in the fog of repeated thoughts about the situation. Over and over, the young scholar had to reconvince himself of the truth behind the outward appearance of his denomination. It was a difficult thing to do. He had to transform his entire view of reality. A new view, a different interpretation of the system he believed in was now necessary.

How had the Apodists kept all their adherents from revealing the secret writings of their inner group? How had they avoided ever raising the curiosity of outsiders not part of their cabal? How had they managed to make themselves so invisible to everyone else?

Why did my parents or my teachers never catch any hint of this subcult? wondered the young man.

He had increasing trouble sleeping at night in his room near the Archivum. His thoughts were burdened with new doubts and emotions.

Ranid sensed growing anger in himself. How could he join the Apod circle and still maintain his self-respect? His personal integrity seemed challenged. He knew that he was incapable of the doubleness and phoniness of having a known and unknown faith co-existing at the same time. Was he going to spend the rest of his life living in duality? The price of what

                CLEMENT S. MASLOFF

the Capitular demanded would be endless self-loathing. He would come to regard himself with withering hatred. The hidden secret would weigh on his sense of what was good.

The young seeker of enlightenment decided that he needed counsel from Praeposter Hyle, staying for hours in his private sanctum. The older man appeared worried and troubled by what had been revealed to them as had his assistant.

Sitting down across from his mentor, Ranid could sense that the older man felt profound unease over their new situation.

"How could I have been so blind not to have perceived any of this?" asked Hyle in an agitated tone. "But now I notice many signs that point in that direction. They were perfect actors, able to put over a fiction that fooled everyone, high or low in status. This conspiracy is unprecedented. The Apodists, well hidden and camouflaged, enjoyed total success until you came along and made these discoveries about the Institutor, Ranid."

"No one need blame themselves," declared the latter. "How could anyone have looked for such a fantastic subterfuge? I myself can only claim to have stumbled on buried secrets. I had no clear purpose in my mind. My lone compass was my unsatisfied curiosity. I searched for one thing and came upon something quite different. But what are we to do now and in the coming days? A decision about that will have to be made before too long. Things cannot remain the way they were before all of this came to light."

Hyle looked at him with sympathy and understanding. "There is no perfect choice, as far as I can see. If the two of us refuse the invitation to join the Apodists, we are both ruined. Who can say how far the Capitular would go to punish and shut us up? Our careers are at an end if we show any resistance. But on the other hand, if we become part of this great conspiracy, we will be no better than the phony characters who perpetuate it. We shall become liars just like them."

"My mind wrestles with the same dilemma," said the younger man. "How can I remain sincerely Salamandrine if I agree to become a part of the secret circle who appear to be in control of our spiritual organization?"

The Praeposter averted his eyes. "I face that question the same way that you do, my friend. Will we have to become the same sort of false Salamandrists as the Capitular and his group of close associates?"

Silence filled the sanctum as both of them pondered these knotty puzzles. Neither, as yet, had specific, definite answers.

Only after a considerable time did Ranid voice a conclusion.

"I can never again see Alsike Caldus the same way I once did."

"Neither can I," muttered the head of the Archivum.

"I am rereading the published writings of the Founder and going through his manuscripts," revealed Ranid. "My aim now is to locate signs or hints of how he handled his spiritual duality. That may eventually help me to deal with the same problem in myself. What do you think of that?"

"Yes, that may turn out to be a pattern we can both imitate."

Hyle proposed that Ranid join him on a hike through the mead around the capital city. It might help them clear their minds for better understanding of their dilemma. Both of them might benefit from such an excursion, they agreed.

The two men crossed a field of brown grass, entering a marsh covered with yellow mullein, purple foxglove, scarlet eyebright, and butter-and-eggs toadflax. Here and there, catkins rose above low spots where eelgrass grew. Ranid looked at the vegetation while Hyle expressed his intimate thoughts and feelings to him.

"I would never try studying the life of our Institutor in detail the way that you have been doing," confessed Hyle. "My knowledge of him was not complete, but it was adequate for practical, day-to-day purposes. There is less curiosity about his human existence than one would suppose. We think that the truth about his life is part of our daily faith. Most Salamandrites do not thirst for broader or deeper knowledge of him. Somehow, they sense that it might be upsetting to them. They feel that they know enough and need no new information. The Founder is treated like a legendary character. No one

                    CLEMENT S. MASLOFF

wishes to discover ordinary human drives or emotions in him. That could result in disappointment and pain.

"Your findings could disorient masses of believers, Ranid."

The young man did not reply at once. As they walked on, he began to talk in a meditative manner, as if only to himself.

"Alsike must have been like only a limited few of the adherents to his doctrines. For me, he was a seeker on an endless quest. There were periods of depression and self-doubt. I believe that he experienced much inner turmoil. For me, he was a gravely troubled explorer of the soul. Alsike was not the average typical man of his time. He had many warring impulses. All of this makes him a difficult person to understand."

Hyle asked him a direct question.

"Would we be wrong to join up with the secret, invisible conspiracy? Perhaps we have no real choice and will be forced to become a part of it, whether we wish to do so or not."

Ranid decided to express himself candidly and bluntly. "For me, it is a matter of personal honor. What integrity would be left me if I compromised my beliefs? My conscience screams out against hypocrisy. How can I preach the principles of Salamandrism, yet hold to another system inside myself? How can I be one thing in private and another before the public? Can the inside and outside selves be opposites? What will be my true identity? No, my choice must be against dualism."

Hyle attempted to dissuade him from drastic rejection. "We have to remember that life is a very practical matter. This duality is not new. It goes back into the early mists of amphibiotic spirituality. There have always been more than a single side to our faith. What does it matter that some honor the frog and others the salamander? These are only intermediaries. There may be a multitude of them. What is the real nature of our differences? How important will they be in terms of eternal time? I doubt that the central essence really varies. The odyle is a single odyle. It can only be one. Why should there be argument and conflict?"

Ranid was astonished at the heretical tolerance and latitudinarian breadth of the Praeposter of the Archivum. He had never expected such opinions to be expressed by the veteran official.

"Are we only play actors in a masquerade, then?" he inquired.

The Praeposter meditated a moment. "I have always been an ambitious individual. Perhaps that makes me a cynic. Despite all doubts, though, I believe we must let the Apodists absorb us. There is no alternative for you and me. It is our duty to accept conditions and circumstances the way they really are."

As Hyle proceeded through the marsh, he suddenly stumbled, losing his balance in a fraction of a second. Not able to regain equilibrium, he collapsed on the ground in sudden, accidental calamity.

Ranid stopped and turned in alarm. Eager to help his companion, he bent down over him. "What happened?" asked the anxious researcher.

"I took a misstep and fell over," explained Hyle. "My left leg is twisted and hurts terribly. I hope it isn't sprained or broken."

"Let me look at it," said Ranid, stooping down and helping the other into a sitting position.

"The pain is horrible," moaned the sufferer. "I'm not sure I can make it back to the capital on my feet." He considered a second. "It may be necessary for you to go to the nearest village for assistance. What do you think?"

Ranid made him as comfortable as he could, then ran down the meadow path. Fortunately, there was a small clachan less than a league away. Not more than a dozen thatched cottages were visible in the small settlement.

As he approached nearer, Ranid had an eerie feeling. A kind of intuition told him that this village might contain Anurans who honored the frog.

Would they refuse any aid to two wandering Salamandrites from the capital city?

     CLEMENT S. MASLOFF

Chapter VII

Approaching the closest structure, Ranid noticed a roof tablet with a green frog painted on it. His premonition had been perfectly correct.

What now?

Ranid decided to knock at this cottage and make a plea for help. There was no time to lose. The unknown condition of Hyle weighed on him. Immediate action was called for, with no hesitation over the difference in faiths.

Several knocks on the betulan door brought forth an old, grizzled man in coarse linsey-woolsey jacket and breeches. The buskins on his feet were of an unidentifiable fabric, some material unfamiliar to Ranid.

"What you want?" said the country character, making an odd grimace.

Ranid tried to be quick and concise. "My walking companion fell and injured his leg. I can't move him by myself."

"He is unable to walk on his own?"

Ranid nodded his head yes.

"I'll call my two sons," said the oldster. "They can carry him to the clachan."

It took only minutes for the pair of husky young farm workers to transport Hyle to their cottage in the village. They lifted him up gently, bearing him in their criss-crossed arms. The father supervised their work. Ranid trailed behind, amazed at their humaneness.

These are Anurans! he had to repeat to himself in his mind.

No one asked the spiritual affiliation of the pair of strangers. But it might have been guessed from subtle, almost invisible signs they themselves were unaware of.

A small grandson of the family elder was sent to fetch the clachan's medicus. This self-taught natural curer determined that Hyle had suffered a broken leg bone.

"You must stay here a few days," decided the folk healer. "Until someone can come to make a cast for your limb. It will take some time before you can walk upright once more."

It was decided by the two city-dwellers that Ranid would go back and report what had happened to the now injured Praeposter. The young man walked all the way to the capital and made a formal report at the Archivum. He then returned to the clachan late in the evening. There was news for him here. The medicus had gone to the district center and brought back an experienced nurser. Together, the two set the leg of Hyle in a temporary plaster cast. That might make an enormous difference in saving his ability to walk.

"We must take this man to the district spitale in the morning," announced the nurser. "They can make him a permanent cast there. That is the best course to take, I would judge."

"I will carry him there in my mule wagon," volunteered the old man who owned the cottage. "He should arrive there as soon as possible."

Soon after dawn, Hyle was carefully loaded into an open farm wagon pulled by an equine. Ranid sat next to the old villager as they slowly journeyed to the central clachan of the area.

The driver assured the pair of strangers that the patient would receive good care at the spitale they were headed for.

"We help each other hereabouts in the marshes," mused the oldster. "Anurans help Salamanders, Salamanders help us. That's the way it is out here."

     CLEMENT S. MASLOFF

Ranid smiled to himself. If only everyone, everywhere were like that.

Since Hyle was unable to walk to the Citadelle, the Capitular himself came to the Archivum to have a talk with him. This was only three days after the accident in the marsh. Caudo Eximius arrived without any retinue, in a gownlike vestimentum of aquamarine. He wore no ensignia of office whatsoever.

Hyle, surprised to find the head of the Salamandrites at the door of his living quarters, ushered him into the apartment cube. The Praeposter moved slowly to his writing desk after asking the high officeholder to take a cohunewood chair.

"I have been informed of your injury and sympathize with you," began Eximius. "It is evident that you are attempting to return to as many of your duties as possible, taking in consideration the problem of mobility. Our hope is for your rapid and full recovery."

"Thank you, sir," smiled Hyle. "I appreciate your concern. The medicos tell me that, in time, my leg will be out of this parget cast and back to normal. Let me say that your coming here is a complete surprise that heartens and encourages me greatly. Thank you, again."

Caudo studied the lines on the face of the Praeposter as if trying to decipher something encoded there. "The young man has returned to his research work?" he softly whispered.

"Yes, he has. Without him having been with me, my physical condition would have been much worse. I am indebted to him for obtaining assistance in time."

The Capitular drew a full, deep breath. "I am here in order to initiate your preparation for membership in our Apodic Brotherhood. The syndics have, on my recommendation, accepted you. We held long discussions about your researcher, Ranid Rolius. The final decision was rejection. He is not the type of person who can be trusted in our small, intimate circle. There is too much risk of harm with him among us. Confidence would be lacking. So, you will be admitted, but not this uncontrollable scholar. To all of us, he appears wild and unpredictable. He is not an individual that we can depend upon with any security. Who can say what new problems he might present in the future?"

Hyle, shaken by these words, groped for some degree of satisfaction.

"Ranid will continue on my staff, doing archival tasks, will he not?"

Eximius seemed to look across at the painted salamanders on the dado of the opposite wall.

"We decided on immediate elimination as the best solution to the problem of this young man. It must be carried out as soon as possible. Do not be alarmed, it will not be the first time we Apods have accomplished anything like that. Over the generations, there have been cases when eradication of potential trouble became necessary. Death has sometimes been meted out to recusants, when there is no other way. Let me tell you about my own involvement.

"When I first entered as a novice Apodist, our circle was experiencing problems with an addicted inebriate. This chronic imbiber came close to revealing secrets several times with his lose talk. But the greatest point of danger was what his wife heard him babble while asleep. You see, the fellow acted as financial treasurer for our Apod Brotherhood. He was in charge of the money relationships between the Salamandrine Organization and our small, secret circle. He knew all aspects of our business, if you understand what I mean. What if he went too far in drunken conversation or nighttime murmuring? It was decided to dispose of the fool, and I was the one appointed to carry out the deadly task. It was a great, heavy responsibility that then rested on my shoulders.

"But how was I to do it? I decided to use a poisonous herb, the widespread one named aconitum. It was easy to purchase a sufficient quantity from a country grower of herbs. I was not at all proud of my deed, but it had to be done. This incident helped me gain the loyalty of the circle, so that when the vacancy occurred it was I who was elected the new Capitular. That killing was the turning point of my entire career, I must confess. It made me who I am and what I am today."

"There is no other way for Ranid?" gulped Hyle in rising consternation.

          CLEMENT S. MASLOFF

"I am afraid not," replied Caudo, his face and his voice icy cold.

Hyle gasped for breath. "When does it happen? And who will be doing it?"

"The fewer who know the particulars of what is going on, the better. I prefer not to use the armed guards, who are outsiders. It must be done inside our own ranks, which you will soon be joining. In a sense, you are a candidate who already knows much about us. So, since you brought him to us, I place this assignment on your shoulders. Do you happen to have any kind of weapon or poison available?"

"No," said the thunderstruck archivist.

"Means can be provided for you this very night. Perhaps a tiny cartridge will do."

"Poison might be easier and more suitable," trembled the Praeposter, engulfed in waves of emotion. "Perhaps the one that you yourself once used."

"I shall send you a vial of aconitum, then. It is fast and deadly. In a short while, my personal famulus will bring it to you."

"The deed must be finished at once?" whispered the quaking Hyle.

"The swifter, the better," replied Caudo with clenched teeth. "I must leave now and see to the matter of the substance you will need."

The Praeposter remained seated as the chief of all Salamandrites departed.

Chapter VIII

Slowly staggering and lurching along an unlighted corridor, Hyle came to the cubiculum of Ranid. Holding onto the crutch he was using for support, he rapped on the quercine door.

The young scholar was surprised to see him. "Come in, sir," he told the injured Praeposter, inviting him to sit on a small, stuffed squab. Ranid himself remained standing.

"I have something urgent to tell you," began Hyle. "This has enormous meaning for your future life. Where shall I begin? Caudo Eximius visited me only a short time ago. He is now gone, but what he said is abominable."

"Abominable?" reacted Ranid with confusion and shock.

"He instructed me to accomplish something that totally disgusts my conscience."

The other drew a step closer. "What could that be?"

Hyle pursed his lips. "I am to see to it that you die. The syndics have rejected you as a recruit to the Apodic Brotherhood, while accepting me. Out of fear that you have dangerous knowledge about their existence, they decided on your immediate elimination. That task is assigned to me, as my first duty to their faith. I am assigned the task of seeing to your destruction.

"They fear eventual public exposure through you. Outsiders might learn of their invisible cult and what it does. A pledge of silence from you would be less than worthless to someone like the powerful Capitular we have ruling over us. Suspicion will always be hanging over your name.

     CLEMENT S. MASLOFF

"There is no longer any place for you within the Salamandrine system, my son. I, of course, refuse to perform this fiendish act. But then he will send someone else, or even kill you himself. There is no place for you any longer in the Archivum. Flight is your only possible escape. And it must happen without a moment of delay. That alone can save you."

"That is incredible!" sighed Ranid, feeling his brain whirl.

"Soon a famulus of Eximius is to bring me the aconitum with which I am to poison you at a refectory meal. It is taken for granted that I shall obey this evil command. That is the method chosen for erasing your further existence."

"What shall I do?" asked the excited Ranid. "Where shall I go?"

"Leave the capital at once. There is one place you can find immediate refuge, among the kind villagers who rescued me. Remember them? The Capitular will surely send people on your trail. But they will keep and protect you there in their clachan. I am certain of that."

"But I am a Salamandrite," objected Ranid, perplexed and confused.

"Not any more, not any longer. These country people, as you saw, are tolerant and warm of heart. They will accept you in their midst. What I think you should do is reveal to them a growing interest in their particular faith. Make them believe that you are thinking of conversion to their way. You have to pose as a potential new Anuran. Do you understand? They will be thrilled by having a city man with a burning interest and curiosity about what they believe. Tell them that you are eager to study and learn, eventually to enter one of their isolated spiritual communities. Do you know what an Anuran coenobium is?"

"That is a group that forms a secluded social island, a retreat for solitude and contemplation. But I would be lying to say that I hope to join one," argued Ranid. "Wouldn't I be a false hypocrite, a dishonest pretender?"

"All that is needed is to profess an interest in their odylology, in a general, philosophic sense. You can say that you seek an opportunity to study their concepts and contemplate in peace and quiet. If you become a student softum in a distant spiritual community, you win for yourself the security and protection of an impenetrable disguise. The matter of final, complete conversion can be left indefinite. They cannot and will not force you, of that I am sure." Hyle paused for a moment. "Aren't our Apodic masters really only pretending to follow the Salandrine teachings? Don't they have a secret system of their own? You can see how fluid and unreal our labels are. So, it is no great misdeed to go among the frog-worshippers and evince an interest in their ideas and methods. It will be most interesting, I assure you. Most importantly, you will be safe in such a place."

"But my flight may cause you terrible harm and trouble, my friend."

Hyle shook his head. "Not at all. I will claim that the aconitum failed to end your life and that, realizing what my intent was, you fled in the night to unknown parts. I will be absolved of any complicity. No one will know what actually happened, that I warned and protected you. Both of us can then give a sigh of relief."

Ranid made a strange grimace, then spoke in candor.

"You shall become a false Apodic, while I go out among the Anurans. At least we both remain some sort of Amphibiots, don't we?" A smile of cynicism crossed his lips.

"That is the price of survival for each of us, my son," muttered Hyle.

Within an hour, the fabulus arrived with the aconitum. By then, Ranid Rolius had deserted the Archivum, taking along with him the two diaries he had discovered there.

During the week he spent among his friends in the clachan near the capital, the fugitive became acquainted with an itinerant Anuran predicator. The aged sermonizer gave the young seeker of truth specific advice about where to continue his efforts for spiritual enlightenment.

"You must go to the province of Salientia. That is the true wetland, in more senses that one. I call it the Batrachian heartland. There are marvelous coenobia there. Enter one of them in order to elevate your soul to a higher plane of life. Identify yourself as one seeking enlightenment. You will learn what you yearn to know in such a place."

"You received your spiritual education there?" inquired Ranid.

     CLEMENT S. MASLOFF

The old man nodded yes. "I have never regretted the time I spent. Neither will you. The experience cannot be described, but it can change your entire life. It will provide you a new purpose and deeper understanding. You shall come to have a greater understanding of both yourself and the spirit of the world we live in."

"What was the name of your community, sir?"

"Feretrum," answered the predicant.

That night, Ranid decided to make that place his destination. But first, he had to get there. Could he make a journey in secret, by unguarded backroads?

Would the local Anurans be willing to shield and aid him?

He announced his decision to the family that was hosting him. They insisted that he stay, but Ranid argued that his future lay in the faraway spiritual community of believers. His new friends accompanied him a few leagues, then left him to proceed alone, on his own. The trekker had only a small map of Caecilia to guide him in the right direction. Specific pathways could be learned en route. He would have to ask questions to guide him onward.

Ranid stopped to rest and study his chart. How did he plan to reach Feretrum in Salientia? There was one extensive obstacle in the way, the delta region around the Salientian River. It would take considerable time and effort to cross that region. Ranid buckled up his courage as he walked forward toward the delta barrier.

The delta had wet forests of basket oak, locust, sugar maple, boxelder, and swamp chestnut. There were also scattered examples of water hickory, shagbark, and live oak. Lakes, lagoons, canebrakes, and muskeg bogs made movement over land difficult. Ranid learned this and much more as he crossed the region's boggy, miry, and fenny areas of unending morass, slough, slime, slosh, mud, and sullage. Dangerous quags, ooze, and swails had to be avoided as he slowly crossed the poachy soil, so hard to judge as to its firmness.

He continually looked behind him, taking an indirect zigzag course to confuse possible pursuers sent by Eximius. Everglade areas were the hardest to traverse. Orange and yellow lantana and tall palmettos created a semi-tropical flavor. Progress grew increasingly difficult for the fugitive.

Almost imperceptibly, he came into a zone of bayous and muskegs. Tule, bulrush, reed mace, horse tail, and cat tail grew out of stagnate waters. Sweet flag, calamus, frog bit, water thyme, and swamp milkweed were visible to the treker as he walked onward. He became familiar with the edibles of the wild, gathering bog bilberries, red whortleberry, and cranberry for occasional snacks along the way.

Ranid whistled to long-legged spoonbills and flycatchers in the waters.

Several times he suspected that a single or several persons were a short distance behind him. Each time he changed direction and thought to give them the slip. Was this all from out of his imagination? There was no way for him to know with certainty. He could not allow himself to become over-confident.

The anxious wanderer entered a district on the periphery of the delta called the Cheerless Swamp. This proved to be undulating wetland forty leagues long and twenty-five wide. Forests here contained cypress, black gum, juniper, swamp cotton gum, and water ash. Patches of marshy grass opened between the stands of trees. An intricate network of bayous provided a maze in which Ranid believed he could lose anyone tailing him. It was a natural labyrinth that would certainly protect him.

The days passed by with his confidence in a successful escape rising as he proved to himself that he could cope with the barriers of nature that stood in his way.

Chapter IX

Increasingly, Ranid passed small clachans where the so-called "swampers" lived. These had to be avoided at all costs, he told himself. It was dangerous to be seen by anyone who could then report him to the pursuers. No such chances were to be taken.

He caught sight of arboreal frogs, the famed flying batrachs of the Cheerless Swamp. Their aerial nests overhung the waters of bayous. At times the young hiker spotted birds native to wet areas: the ibis, heron, egret, bittern, boatbill, grassquit, fringilla, crested seriema, yellow-hammer, brambling, and seedeater. These creatures showed no fear of him whatever. They appeared to be ignoring him, knowing that he was only passing by them and would be gone.

Flying insects continually pestered the tired walker: ephemera, dipterons, aedes, and cullices. At night, as he rested in a sleeping bag, the cicala sounded from afar and nearby. Several times he came upon raccoons and muskrats. Once a pair of hunters with long shooting arms crossed his path without seeing him. He was glad there was no occasion to talk with them.

The landscape slowly changed, though. He saw more grass trees, fringe trees, tupelos, and black gums. Fields of rice and sugar cane appeared. Diving coots and scoters became common in ponds and lagoons. Waterweed, club moss, lycopods, asphodels, and meadowsweet grew predominant. Ranid picked and ate wild pieplant and rhubarb, along with juneberry and serviceberry. Orange-flowered butterfly weed and red bloodroot gave the bogs a strange beauty that captivated the fancy of the fugitive scholar. Swamp marigold and kingcup thrilled him with their luxurious brightness of color. He marched by them as if in a trance.

The ground started to become spongy and water-logged. Ranid had to tread forward carefully over layers of peat, recognizing the danger of sudden bog-slides. The unwary could quickly be buried. The time had come, he realized, to find a clachan where food was available for purchase. But where was it best to replenish his supplies? he asked himself in desperation. How would he know whether the local residents were trustworthy and safe to deal with?

His decision was to enter the first hamlet that gave him a sense of safety.

Early after dawn, as the swamp mist was dissipating, he took his chance, ambling boldly down the single street of an obscure, isolated clachan.

Two swampmen in brown twill approached him, one from the right, the other from the left. The outsider stopped, expecting inevitable questioning by them.

"Are you looking for something, brother?" said a tall, skinny man with a brimless hat on his head. "Perhaps we can be of help to you."

"I am on a long journey and need to buy some food to carry with me," replied the stranger from the capital. "I am able to pay for everything that is provided me. My hope is that someone will agree to supply me what I need."

"Come with us," directed the second local. "We will take good care of you."

Walking off between the pair, Ranid realized that these were Anurans in a village of the same. He knew it intuitively. What would it mean for him, though? How would the residents treat him?

The three came to a reed hut where the lanky swamper knocked. A short, round man opened the plank door. His hydrargyrum eyes fastened on the stranger in the middle.

"This man is seeking to buy some food," said the tall, thin local. "I thought you might wish to deal with him, Tadige."

The owner of the small reed cottage stood aside so that the unknown man could enter the shadowy front room. Neither escort followed him in.

"Please, take a seat," said the fat man. The two sat down on rough hassocks with cushions filled with bird feathers.

The man who had been addressed as Tadige offered his visitor a saucer full of planera nuts. "No, thank you," said Ranid, instantly regretting his refusal. When would he again have anything as solid to eat? he wondered.

"You must be from far away," gently declared the villager. "I can tell by the way that you speak. You are not of our region or area."

"Yes, I am from the capital city, Caecilia. The Cheerless Swamp is absolutely new and unfamiliar for me. It is not at all as easy to traverse as I earlier supposed. The swampland has many hazards that one must avoid in order to cross it in safety."

Tadige peered intently at the outsider from elsewhere.

"Are you fleeing something?" he unexpectedly asked.

Ranid was unable to conceal his confusion and distress at this point. "Why do you say that to me? Do I look like a person running away? What makes you think so?"

The other gave a knowing sort of smile.

"I can catch certain signs that few see. My power of interpretation has always been a high one. From the first moment, it seemed to me that you are trying, with enormous effort, to conceal inner anxiety of mind and nerves. There is a serious tension within your soul, not hard at all for me to detect.

"But do not at all be afraid. Patrollers rarely come here, for we are quite remote. You are safe in our clachan from official snoopers. We have nothing for them to pry into. And our people include no active busybodies. So, there is nothing for you, sir, to be afraid of among us. Nothing at all, I assure you."

A sudden idea flashed into Ranid's head. "Can I find a place to stay in your clachan? I am exhausted and need considerable rest. All expenses will be paid, I promise."

Tadige did not need time to consider.

"I myself own a small, unoccupied cottage on the edge of a nearby muskeg. At present, my only use for it is to store the anil I collect for indigo dye. I can rent it for whatever you wish to give me. I hope that it satisfies your needs and taste."

"It will. I assure you it will."

"Good," nodded the swampman. "You and I shall go to see it at once."

Ranid became acquainted with the life of the people of the clachan, but carefully limited any information about himself. Yes, he had been born and raised a Salamandrite, but his spiritual views were larger and broader. Experience had made him tolerant and unprejudiced. He longed to learn more about the Anuran concepts and way of thinking. His mind was open to new spiritual ideas and interpretations.

Ranid had to walk carefully across gazon and grass turf, avoiding the mud holes referred to as loblollies. He joined the swampmen in the gathering of wild oxhearts, spiceberries, checkerberries, partridgeberries, sapodilla plums, and breadfruit. Exploration of the low, marshy swales of the area occurred, with Tadige as his guide.

The latter related his happy-go-lucky philosophy of life to the newcomer.

"Everything we do or strive for depends on the lucky chance," he expostulated. "It is the happy fluke that produces happiness, it is the windfall that gives good fortune. Why do we honor and revere the batrach frogs? Long ago our forefathers discovered that frogs are the most apotropaic of all the amphibians. They enjoy special favor with the spirit of the odyle. The world is as simple as that.

"Let me tell you a story about an uncle of mine. Today, he is dead and long gone. But when he was alive everyone could hear him curse against the frogs of the delta. He complained they kept him awake at night with their loud croaks. And they invaded the garden that he cultivated for himself. Yes, he railed at them as noisome pests that ate his food and interrupted his sleep.

     CLEMENT S. MASLOFF

"So what happened to this uncle of mine?"

"Tadige made a dramatic halt in his narrative at this point.

"He ate some wild caprifigs that killed him rapidly," he said with a grin. "But our local folk healer claims it was really frog fever that did him in.

"Who can say?"

Ranid soon made most of the tiny community his friends. He learned their interpretation of orthodox Anuranism, a simplified version taught to him by Tadige.

He learned to refer to the local frogs as grenouillians and the toads as crapaudics, the way that the villagers did.

Chapter X

"I am a seeker of truth, wherever it can be uncovered," Ranid said to Tadige one evening in the latter's cottage.

The young fugitive described his disillusionment with the leaders of the Salamandrites."There is terrible hypocrisy in their higher circles, I have witnessed it with my own eyes. It is a discouraging situation."

"No one anywhere can carry out and fulfill the highest spiritual ideals," asserted Tadige. "Whether of one denomination or the other, no human can reach the highest pinnacle. That is impossible for even the best of us. You will understand that as you grow older, my friend. But we must never despair of progressing, or stop learning more about the odyle and its visible face in this world." He stopped for a time, then resumed again. "Have you ever seen a prosoponic mask?"

The young man admitted that he had not.

"I will show you mine."

The host rose and moved to the back of the cottage. He then returned holding a bright green object in his hands.

"This mask, given me by my father, has been passed on for almost two hundred years. So, this is a very old symbol of adhesion to the Anuran faith. And these masks, shared by the oldest families, have a deep meaning. When this is put on and worn during a holiday, it stands for a prosopic union of the odyle with our sacred frog. It makes us think about our own prospective union with the highest spirits when our lives come to an end. This is the face of an odyllic frog.

   CLEMENT S. MASLOFF

"Some day, when you complete long studies, you can be granted a prosoponic mask of your own. But the requirements are very high and demanding. Do not cease, my boy, until you win your own mask.

"The best way to reach that plane of achievement is by entering one of our coenobia, the special settlements of those seeking enlightenment. That is the path I hope that you take, Ranid. It will lead you to sublime illumination in both your mind and your spirit."

Yes, the visitor meditated. That has become my life's dream, too.

Ranid realized that it was no longer only a matter of finding a safe haven. His goal now transcended personal security. There was within his mind a growing thirst of curiosity about the faith of the Anurans. He saw it in a light never experienced by him before. Though still occupying a Salamandrine base, he was starting to explore uniquely different spiritual territory that held an unexpected fascination for him.

He had become an explorer in territory that had earlier seemed alien and unfriendly to him. His Salamandite education had taught him fear and revulsion toward the people who had befriended and sheltered him.

His view of the Anurans had been completely reversed through contact with them. He now identified with them and the lives they led.

There was no warning the morning that the patrollers in orange uniforms arrived. They went from cottage to cottage, asking questions about any strangers seen. A half dozen drawings of criminals' faces were shown to the inhabitants of the clachen. No one made any identification, although one countenance that was pictured was a quite familiar person. Everyone kept silent about it.

Ranid received a message in time, so that he succeeded in hiding on the far side of a local lagoon. He stayed there in a swamp grove till dark, when Tadige came to inform him that the patrollers were finally gone. He could now return to the spare cottage he was using, for the time being.

The two men discussed the grave situation as they walked back to the clachan together.

"Someone reported having seen a stranger some leagues away, moving in this direction. For all we know, it might have been some other person, but not you. There are always people fleeing into these parts. The patrollers were trying to confirm the rumor. All of us said that we had seen no one and knew nothing. We have no traitors in our midst. All of us know you and cannot consider you a criminal. We recognized the charge against you to be false."

"What was it, may I ask?"

"The accusation was nonsense about embezzlement from an archive. You are supposed to have taken some historical documents away with you. But we can all vouch for your honesty, if we had to. I take it that the Salamandrian officials are the ones persecuting you."

"That is the truth, Tadige."

The pair came to the cottage where Ranid was staying. They halted, facing each other.

"What shall I do now? They will surely be back here. Has the time arrived for me to travel onward?"

"If you are to leave us, it must be quickly. There is no time to lose, for your safety."

The swampman stared through the darkness at the fugitive. "I believe you should go to the district centrum and find refuge at the Anuran fane there. I will accompany you and introduce you to the missioner in charge of the templum. He is a person of solid integrity and can be trusted. But your departure for the centrum must be tonight. There can be no delay."

"I must pack my things at once, then," said Ranid. "It will take me only a little while to get ready. I will, of course, miss you and the clachan all my life."

The two stared at each other in silence for a moment.

"I have preparations to make for our night trek," smiled Tadige. "I shall return here in half an hour or so. Then, we go to the centrum to hand you over to Frater Joal."

Ranid did not happen to ask why his companion carried a backpack. It seemed to be an empty one. Not until they reached their destination did he learn what was in it.

After hours of treading swamp trails, the district's central village appeared.

Tadige, leading the way, stopped and turned toward the second man. He spoke to him in a soft, intimate whisper. "I have something in my pack that I wish to give you. It will remind you, in the future, of your stay in our clachan. My hope is that it will also encourage your further study and advancement in the faith I hold."

He bent over and removed the backpack, placing it on the ground, then opening the flap.

Ranid watched him in awe. What was this about? Then he saw what Tadige pulled out for him to see. It was the ancestral prosopic mask with the frog's face.

"I cannot take that from you," stammered Ranid. "It has been in your family for generations, for many years. Who am I to go off with such an heirloom?"

The swamper gave a laugh. "I have too many sons, and cannot possibly leave it to all of them. So, if you take it as our gift, much brotherly strife in the future will be nicely avoided. Do you understand me? Taking it will be a favor to my family after I am gone. Do not insult me with a refusal."

"Very well, then," said the wanderer, taking the green mask in his hand.

Tadige helped him to store it away in the large backpack, where he kept the two diaries from the Archivum.

Traversing a swamp grove of dense trees, Ranid occupied his mind identifying the regional birds he had already come to know. His sharp eye caught sight of the fabled lovebird, the ortolan, lorikeet, spotted peetweet, peahen, perdix, trichoglass, and brush-tongued lorry. I have become a traveling birdwatcher! the fugitive told himself. Indeed, this journey of escape to safety had allowed a number of noticeable transformations in him. All of nature now seemed to have meaning as its infinite aspects revealed themselves to him. Why had there never been this wide interest within his mental apparatus? Everything seemed fresh and crisp. His senses were newly born, with unprecedented impressions making their way through them to his innermost mind.

A black and green tree snake stuck out its lengthy tongue from an encinal oak, frightening an olive brown and blue kea to take instant flight into the cloudless sky.

Ranid avoided stepping on a testudo, seeing its grass-colored tortoise shell in time.

As he carefully proceeded onward, his nose caught the strong odor of a fraxinella bush. But within only seconds there came the pleasureable scent of a spicebush.

In the short time until the two left this area of trees, Ranid noted fiddlewood, devilwood, basswood, and satinwood. He had learned to distinguish them accurately by individual traits.

But, from time to time, his thoughts returned to his future course.

How was he going to span the gulf from his Salamandrine past into a different type of existence? Where was this quest of his taking him? Curiosity was propelling him on an unpredictable path impossible to chart ahead of time.

Chapter XI

A cute zircon eyes took in the stranger from the capital of Caecilia.

The missioner was a large bear of a man named Joai, dressed in a long, coarse gunny gown.

Tadige had left to return home after bringing Ranid to the striawood frame-house where the cleric lived. Upon hearing the story of the trials and persecution of the young man, the frater offered him refuge under his own roof. He studied the fugitive with steady, unblinking eyes. "You wish to learn our systematic odylology?" he asked Ranid.

"Yes. All my life, from early childhood, I have had a consuming curiosity about the realm of the spiritual. There is no way of foretelling where my intellectual explorations might take me, but I am compelled by everything within me to continue the already started journey. I need guidance and advice where to go next. Would you be willing to become my mentor?"

The frator nodded his head. "Certainly. I would be delighted to do so. It is evident to me that you have already made a good start. I can teach you the principles of metaphysical study that I learned during my years at Feretrum. That is the famous conventicle community where I acquired my education. We can use the same standard manuals from there that are still taught. I keep them for references in my sermons. They are an excellent instrument for the mastering of our central principles. They can guide your study quite well, believe me."

"I am prepared to begin at once," smiled Ranid with joy on his face.

"You should rest first," said the missioner. He rose and led his student to a small bedroom upstairs. In seconds, the tired newcomer was asleep on a truckled pallet.

Ranid rose early, rested and ready to begin something new.

Joai, already sitting in the kitchen, had set a breakfast of small bird ovula and bright red rambutan fruit. Even while they ate, the pair went forward into the subjects that most concerned them.

"You will find that our system is rich and subtle in its complications. But it is completely orderly. Every part fits together perfectly. I do not like making comparisons, but we Anurans have from the beginning been the foremost creators of a universal conceptual structure. You shall see that with your own eyes as you read the book I am going to assign for reading and study. Our logical system is incomparable. It contains unified strength and harmony.

"The best starting point is that of the quiddity of the odyle, the essence of the spiritual foundation of all existence. Can you tell me what a quid is? Have you ever come across that term or idea before?" asked Joai.

"No," confessed the guest as he continued eating. "It is totally new to me."

"Quids are the ultimate components of the universe, the individual parts that are the smallest and indivisible. They have no shape of their own, no extension or dimensions. Their essence is their spiritual being. If I had to characterize their nature, it is to act and move. They are the centers of all the operating forces in existence. But they do not act upon each other. Not at all. The actions of each quid exclude those of every other one. They exist to themselves and by themselves. The motion of each quid results from its own past motions, almost like inertia. Every quid is the determiner of its own future. No other factor is such, not even the odyle. I plan for you to find out how these quids hang together, though each is separate and independent."

Ranid, finishing his breakfast, concentrated now on answering his host.

   CLEMENT S. MASLOFF

"You speak of contradiction between the concepts of the odyl and the quid, but I believe it is only an apparent one. What if the little quids are only microcosmic mirrors reflecting the universal odyl? And the primary quid is an overarching amphibian, such as the frog or the salamander? So that every quid that exists has internal images that are the shadow of the odyl. What does this amphibian factor accomplish in the picture of reality? Perhaps it is a lens through which every separate, autonomous quid sees and senses the odyl."

Surprisingly, Joai gave a happy grin. "I must say, Ranid, that you possess an extremely agile philosophical mind. And you have not even begun serious metaphysical study yet. I foresee enormous progress ahead. You are a wonder, in my estimation. Who could have predicted that such a gifted young thinker would come to me for spiritual instruction? It will make me extremely happy to guide you through the landscape of our Anuran system of thought and understanding."

The pair gazed at each other with rising, expanding hope.

⸺

Ranid read Anuran books for several days. Joai continued to quiz his pupil at their meals together. The questions grew sharper and more difficult.

"By itself, the Absolute is distant and abstract. How can the Sublime become specific and concrete?"

"A tangible medium is necessary," assured Ranid. "A being that humans can see and touch, an intermediary through which people can contact the original energy of all the universe, the odyle of everything."

"Yes," reacted the missioner with satisfaction. "Our sacred frog brings the Ultimate close to us, so that it is now tangential. None of us need ever be alone again. There shall be a higher form of being always with us, wherever we be."

Ranid went on with the thought. "Life has a new meaning when we are able to connect ourselves to the odyle. I have come to recognize the infinite value of the tie to the highest spirituality. It is the supreme goal of all life."

"What do you know about the nature of the soul?" asked the Frater all of a sudden.

The student searched his memory for a moment.

"Since all existents are only ideas in the mind of the odyl, our souls have to be ideas also. Yes, my soul is an identifiable idea of the Absolute called the odyl. That is what it is."

Joai sprang up from his chair. "I see that your knowledge is already extensive. As a result, we can enter directly into advanced topics and areas. There is no need to wait. You are ready to go forward to the frontier of our system of thought. There is no need to wait any longer.

"You will go on to a volume on the Prosopon of the odyle. Do you know what that means? It is the face of the Sublime, personified in the batrachian frog. The process is termed Prosopopeia. It is how the odyl creates its own face out of itself. It is the development of a medium from out of the Absolute. You see, if a human has made a union with the sacred frog, that is also a simultaneous union with the odyl as well. Prosopic union is possible in a state of mental ecstasy. It is called spiritual ebriety back there in Feretrum." He stopped a second. "I am getting ahead of myself. Mystical exercises are a final plane of study. We shall proceed with more subordinate subjects now. Later, I will relate what is known about direct spiritual union."

Ranid found himself taking daily lessons in the Anuran literature. His reading centered on works from Feretrum that utilized deictic, elenctic, and apodeictic methods of argument and logic. He learned to define the odyle as the divine alembic that refines, purifies, and transforms its chosen object by giving it the deipotent nod of favor. And this supreme numen in the world was the chosen amphibian, the frog of Caecilia. His study revealed the supernatural transfiguration by which the batrachian medium of the frog was elevated to becoming the physical face of the odyle. It was an extremely compelling and cogent argument that was made to him.

Joai gave his pupil access to his manuals of liturgics. Ranid rapidly picked up the litanies, invocations, incantations, appeals, applications, entreaties, petitions, prayers, and chants of the Anuran templa. He began to attend

   CLEMENT S. MASLOFF

frog services at the small fane located near the house of the missioner. One day, in his second month of studies, his teacher made a surprise request of Ranid.

"You have a fine, rich voice, my friend. Would you be willing to act as my precentor? There has never been anyone here knowledgeable enough to read the lessons and chant the responses. I think you are now fully capable of becoming my psalmodist in the temple services I lead. It would be wonderful if you became an active participant of our continual spiritual practices. I would be overjoyed to have you assisting me in our daily services."

Ranid accepted, thereby becoming the vocal chanter of the local congregation.

The sonorous voice of the stranger was soon talked about by the inhabitants of the centrum. People who had not been to the fanum in years now attended to hear his melodious tones in hymns to the frog. The building rang with the echoes of his strong baritone. People enjoyed hearing him sing, recite, and read aloud. His participation was a glowing success. He became a star attraction in the services.

Ranid became acquainted with an ever widening circle of members and visited the weekly centrum market, where the swamp people brought food items to sell. The young man from the capital grew familiar with the wares displayed there, so many of which were new to him. For meat-eaters, there was terrapin, anguine, cacomistle, coati, and daman. In the fruit section, Ranid discovered rambutan, nepal, genipap, capsicum, sweetsop, maypop, crowberry, bearberry, dogberry, naseberry, and soapberry.

The cuisine of the Cheerless Swamp fascinated the curious scholar with its uniqueness and originality.

It was while at one of these weekly markets that the fugitive spotted two suspicious-looking outsiders who caused him immediate alarm.

Chapter XII

The pair of intruders were wearing city coats of bright, gaudy color, not the local dark cloth. The first thought of Ranid was that these were undercover scrutinizers, working for either the official police or the Salamandrine authorities. He quickly slipped away and hurried home, a lump of fear in his throat. What was he to do now? He decided to inform Joai of the problem that he faced with the arrival of these strangers from elsewhere.

The missioner was busy in his kitchen, baking corndoggers. Ranid waited until the bread rolls were in the wood oven before revealing the danger that threatened his freedom.

Joai looked at him with startlement and disbelief. "You think they may be spying agents of your Salamandrian persecutors?"

"That seems most likely to me," answered Ranid. "There was something about them that told me they were on the hunt for someone. I could not draw any other conclusion."

The missioner furrowed his broad brow. "What do you intend to do, then?" he asked.

"I can't stay indoors all the time. My fear is that they will corner me right here, and that will therefore cause a lot of trouble for you and your templum."

Joai bit his thick lower lip. "I know of only one safe haven for you, one secure refuge where they cannot trail you."

"What is that?"

     CLEMENT S. MASLOFF

The Anuran mentor looked down at the pale citron linoleum floor.

"The conventiculum at Feretrum is the best asylum I can think of for you. No police can enter it. Because I was once a student there, my recommendation will count for a lot. But the journey there is a long, difficult one. There can be many hardships. Are you willing to travel that far on your own?"

"I swear to you that I am," replied Ranid with a glow of sincerity and honesty.

"Their main purpose at Feretrum is the study and preservation of the Anuran faith. There are many colonies of actual frogs raised and maintained, out of which beneficial medicines are sold and sent to healers and members of the general public." Joai thought and considered a moment. "I could send you as a candidate for noviciate status. Are you willing to enroll yourself? It is a tough, arduous life for a beginner there. Are you up to its rigors?"

Without hesitation, Ranid said that he was ready to go to Feretrum and become a student of Anuranism. His most cherished personal aspirations could be realized by such a course of education. It would be the next logical step in his spiritual development. He was willing and eager to go there and learn what was so important to him.

"Good!" proclaimed Joai. "It will be a sad loss for me, but this must be done for your sake. Pack up what you need and be prepared to leave the centrum tonight. That will be the best time to slip away.

"I shall now go to my escritoire and write a strong letter introducing you and giving my positive evaluation of your worth and promise. My regrets are great, but this is necessary for your future. You will find a true shelter and salvation once you reach Feretrum."

Ranid saw tears forming in the eyes of the missioner who had become so close to him. He left the kitchen, soon finding himself beginning to cry himself.

～

Ranid was ready to leave the house of Joai as soon as twilight fell. He waited in the rear of the building, in a small storage nook, until he heard the front door open. Bending forward, the fugitive put his ear to the door separating him from the front parlor. The missioner had let two persons in. They had to be the pair of pursuers who were after him. He listened to the audible words in a low, heavy voice of one of the intruders.

"We know that you harbor a stranger to this centrum, and from what we can gather it sounds a lot like the man we are hunting for. This criminal stole valuable manuscripts from the archive in Caecilia City. The felony is most serious, because these articles are irreplaceable. He will be given the highest possible punishment when he is caught and returned to the capital. His offense damaged the peace and well-being of all people in our land. I cannot give you a detailed description of the contents of these purloined materials, for we do not know them. But we have the name of this miscreant, Ranid Rolius. And we have a very good idea what the evil malefactor looks like. I can show you a drawn sketch of this horrible criminal."

Silence followed as the scrutinizer took the picture out of his pocket and handed it to Joai. The latter studied and then returned it and began to speak.

"No, this is not the student that I have been tutoring. The two are completely different in looks and body types. You are barking up the wrong tree, sirs."

"Tell me one simple thing," said the senior agent. "Where is this person who stays here wih you?"

"He is not now at home. I do not expect him till some time late tomorrow, because he is on a hiking tour, on a hunt for wild berries. The youth is fascinated with the rich variety we have in this part of the Cheerless Swamp. I am very sorry, but if you wish to examine him with questions, it has to be done tomorrow. At what hour do you expect to return here to the house?"

Ranid was unable to hear the reply to this, if there was one.

The next sound reaching his ears was that of the front door opening and closing. The one being hunted felt relief. They had been unable to search the house for him because it was clear to them that Joai would refuse to grant them permission for that.

     CLEMENT S. MASLOFF

Ranid made his way into the front parlor to consult with his protector.

"I must leave at once, this night," proposed the young fugitive. "There is no use in presenting these men the opportunity to catch hold of me. Perhaps it would be best to go directly into the swamp by the most direct route, from the back of this house. I have my knapsack packed and can start off at once. My best wishes for the future are all that I can leave you, my dear friend. So, let us shake hands and say farewell to each other."

Joai approached and placed his hands around the shoulders of the other.

All at once, the missioner remembered something.

"Before you depart, there is a gift I have to give you. What is there here that you could use? I asked myself that question. A book, I decided. But which one? Let me get it for you so that you can see."

Joai took only seconds to go to a shelf and take out a single book. He brought it over and handed it to his student. The latter opened the volume and read what the title was: "History of the Origin of the Anuran Faith".

"This will help you understand how the Great Schism occurred, especially the role played by the famous Alsike Caldus. The character of his treachery is described and defined. The book tells of how he plotted to take a large number of faithful believers out of the united, consolidated Anuran movement. You will read about the Unity Congress, where Batrachians and Salientians tried to merge their separate strains of frog and salamander priority into one unified organization.

"The historical convention was held in Caecilia City. Ever since that time, there has persisted the dispute over who caused the total division. Did the Anurans split from the Salamandrites, or vice versa? Who instigated the final, total division?

"The book that I am giving you tells the truth about the final schism and how it happened. It places the blame for the separating conflict on one person: Caldus the troublemaker. Reading it will bring you important enlightenment, Ranid."

The latter took the small volume and placed it into his knapsack.

After the two embraced each other, the fleeing one exited through the rear door of the house at nearly a run.

Chapter XIII

Ranid followed a diagram that sketched the way to Feretrum. This was the only map he possessed. It was clear to him that the journey was to be a long, circuitous one. The fleeing trekker was on an indirect route away from the larger centers. There was no way for him to foresee where his pursuers might lurk in order to capture him. He had to take every conceivable precaution to avoid the enemy, regardless of the amount of time wasted in doing so. This was not going to be an easy trip for him, not at all. He recognized the severity of what would be done to him if he was captured.

When he stopped at noontime to eat some of the food that Joai had packed in his knapsack, Ranid glanced through the Anuran history he had been given. He turned to the chapter dealing with the Unity Congress in the capital, and the part that Alsike Caldus played in its break up into schismatic divisions. This was a period and a topic never covered in detail in any Salamandrine work that he had ever read. It would, of course, be an Anuran interpretation of events, but it promised to contain views of absorbing interest for him. Burning curiosity led him to plow through the section in which the Salamandrine Institutor and Founder appeared on the stage of history as a decisive actor.

"The Batrachian delegates, fated to become the Anurans, came predominantly from the northern and eastern regions of Caecilia. The Salientians who turned into the Salamandrites tended to be from the south and west of the country. Preliminary discussions seemed to indicate that most of the major problems and differences had already been solved and settled, or would be compromised at the Congress. An agreement had been reached on the question of placing toads within the system to be enacted by majority vote. These bufonic relatives of the frog were to be put on the same level as the ranic tadpoles and treated as frogs in future times. Toads were meant to enjoy new honor and higher position than ever before.

"There appeared to be no major difficulty on the horizon until the fiery address of Alsike Caldus, spokesman for the most stubborn salamander faction. He and his followers caused the explosive division that put an end to any prospect of unity. Alsike was the major instigator of the final conflict that resulted in the split and separation.

"He was an individual unknown to most of those attending the Congress. What is his business with us? inquired many when he asked for the floor and started to give an harangue against the unity direction most of the delegates appeared to be taking. His tirade berated the organizers of the convention as devious political operators seeking greater power and control over members' resources. This orator, Caldus, coming out of nowhere, gave a diatribe against leaders of unification, especially the Anurans striving for harmony and concord. His speech grew malicious and abusive. He barely knew the targets of his vitriolic attacks, yet he made personal attacks on them as individuals. His animosity was directed against both the frog and the toad factions, for he feared Anuran unity as a threat to his own plans and strategy.

"Finally, after he sat down and surrendered the floor, a motion was made to censor the man's hateful words. This passed almost unanimously. By then, the offender of the rules of civil decency had already left the Congress and Caecilia City. He began an all-out campaign for division and separation, founding new temples and mission offices throughout the country. His attacks on the newly created Anuran organization became ever more vicious. A schismatic movement based upon salamander-worship took shape with Caldus as its leader and architect. Its central theme was the splitting tactics of the hater who stood at its helm. Alsike Caldus failed in his chief purpose of destroying the Great Consolidation of all Batrachians with the toad-based Salientians. The Unity Congress had repudiated his attempt to break up the emerging Anuran consensus. His reaction was to lead the Salamandrites into absolute schism and division, out on their own. That was the terrible result of his malicious machinations."

Ranid, his brain in a spin, closed the history volume and placed it back in his knapsack. What was he to make out of what he had just read? It completely contradicted what he had learned from his Salamandrine education. First of all, his previous understanding had been that it was Caldus and the Salamandrites who had summoned the Unity Congress. They had supposedly called Amphibiots of every stripe to the general conclave. No prior conditions or requirements had been set. Division came about when the Batrachians tried to exclude anyone except frog and toad partisans from participating. The initial split originated with the newly formed Anuran coalition, according to what he had been taught throughout his education years. It was Alsike who had supported an all-inclusive consolidation, he had long believed, not his frog-centered enemies.

Now he was reading how the newly formed Anurans were the true systematizers, the builders of a logical cooperation. Alsike and his Salamandrites were depicted as confused mystics driven by spiritualistic emotion and political tactics into divisive conflict and schism. They were the heretical troublemakers, according to this interpretation new to him. It was breathtaking, but also puzzling, to the reader of this history.

This Anuran version of what happened stood on its head the one that had been inculcated into his brain by his teachers and superiors.

Ranid grinned sadly and forlornly.

How was his overloaded mind going to deal with these historical riddles?

As he placed the knapsack on his shoulders and set off on the trail once more, his hopes for clarification focused on the coenobium that was his destination. After this long, difficult trek of his through the swamps, he hoped to find answers at the great Anuran center ahead of him.

Walled and secluded, Feretrum stood on a high hummock above the swamps and marshes of the region called Salientia. This was a zone of frogs and toads, in both a geographical and spiritual sense. Small lakes and ponds, wetlands and bayous abounded here. The heart of Anuranism was located in this paludial portion of Caecilia.

Ranid Rolius was on edge as he approached the entrance gate of the coenobium. He had learned from the locals that the Mandator of the spiritual community was a man named Keigo Tragus. Would that person accept him as a student softum? Ranid knew that his future depended on convincing the ruling abbatial to admit him as a pupil. On his own, he had to conceal and suppress the memory of his previous life in the capital. He had to erase the remnants of his Salamandrine education and activity. Whatever he said had to be credible to this head man, Keigo Tragus. Nothing would be possible without a successful philosophical disguise that hid the nature of his own past.

From a large stand of bluetrees came the distinctive song of hirundines and pratincoles, mingled with the distinctly different tones of a swamp snakebird.

A conventicler in orange gown walked toward him as he neared the quercine door at the gate. Ranid gave his name and the tall member led him inside the walled refuge.

A number of brothers were engaged in games of spillikin, throwing down and picking up jackstraws made of silken grogram.

Several structures that resembled barracks stood in parallel, right-angled formation. All at once, Ranid's guide stopped before the door of one of them.

"The Abbad will see you inside the bedehouse. Go right in, he is expecting your arrival."

Ranid did as told, opening the door of the low building and entering. He moved carefully down an unlighted corridor toward an illuminated chamber at the end. As he neared the end, a ringing voice sounded forth from out of it.

"Come in, I've been awaiting you all this morning."

The room that Ranid stepped into was somewhat small, yet packed with books, document rolls, and data reels on wall shelves and in storage boxes. Behind a low gopherwood desk sat a plump, rotund man with a bald head and clear emerald eyes. "Please sit down," said the officeholder in a quiet, controlled tone.

The fugitive took a yellowwood chair opposite the Mandator of Feretrum. He suddenly realized that his face and the expression on it was being watched by the chief of the entire coenobium. What was Tragus perceiving from his outer aspect? How penetrative was the man's mind?

The Anuran leader began to speak in a moderated, muffled vocal register.

"Why is it that you wish to join us? Can you tell me that?"

Ranid tried to follow the outline he had prepared in his mind, but found that impossible.

"I have since childhood been on a quest of the spirit. As far back as my memory goes, there has been this burning, excruciating hunger for enlightenment within me. A search for the infinite, the eternal, I sometimes call it. What can I say? It is difficult to be more specific, more definite than that. But that has been the drive and the aim of my whole life."

"I think that I understand," muttered the other with the hint of a smile on his lips. "But why here, why come to Feretrum? There are other places and locations, other conventicula. Why did you choose us to be your spiritual nest?"

Thrown off balance by a question not foreseen, Ranid realized he had to extemporize.

"I know my own weaknesses, Abbad. They are many. It is often difficult for me to maintain whatever resolution I make. Distractions are always present. They appear often and have an easy time diverting me. I have heard that Feretrum has the formal strictness that my character needs and demands. I do not desire to be in any laxer coenobium. My soul needs a solid, demanding discipline."

The candidate for entrance looked into the sharp emerald eyes, trying to read there whether his unrehearsed explanation was having any success.

"That is interesting," smiled the old man. "No brother has ever said that he came here for the sake of our hard life and severity. You are the first one to do so, my son. But we must feed you before a decision is made about your future. My famulus will see that you eat first, then we shall resume our interesting conversation with each other."

The Mandator pulled a chord that summoned his personal servant to appear and take the candidate to a nearby dining chamber.

 CLEMENT S. MASLOFF

Chapter XIV

"I realize that you wish me to speak candidly, sir," said Ranid to the Mandator at their second meeting in late afternoon. "My past spiritual experience was within the boundaries of Salamandrism, and it ended in great pain and confusion for me. I had to conclude that it was impossible to continue that way. So, my only alternative was to start exploration of the opposite major faith system. I have already studied Anuranism with a local predicant and then with a missioner. But the more I learned, the more I sensed a need to go further in my exploration. Does that seem logical to you? My journey of the spirit has only begun. So, I made a decision to come to Feretrum for my inner edification. My advisors all informed me that Feretrum was my best hope of full enlightenment for my mind and soul."

"We prize such truthfulness as you have expressed to me," said Tragus musingly. "Tell me this: do you have metaphysical curiosity about odylogical questions?"

"Indeed I do," answered Ranid, growing excited and animated. "Such topics fascinate me. Abstract fundamentals often hypnotize me. My mind is always dwelling upon primal theory. I dream of the fullest understanding possible."

It seemed that at this point the Mandator spoke as if from a high, distant elevation. "I have always considered myself a contemplator, a thinker more than an official or authority. Even today, my evenings are taken up with reading and writing. My main interest has always been in studying the odyle and finding out how to construct a direct relationship to the Absolute. From my starting days, that has been my special concentration."

"My own curiosity has been drawn to that same area," confessed the younger man.

Tragus stared fixedly at him.

"I believe you are an acceptable candidate to join us as a softum," said the Mandator. "We need people of your caliber and interests in our conventiculum. I intend to take direct charge of your study and training. There are too many time-servers and careerists among us. A person with such a strong philosophical dimension could be quite valuable to us. As you know, we have both married and unmarried members of both sexes in our community. Years ago I met my own spouse here at Feretrum. She passed away when my daughter was only a child. My Glia lives with me and is something of a philosophizer herself." His face suddenly darkened into a gloomy shadow. "She is all that I have, and I am everything to her. It is difficult for a young woman in a community like ours, predominantly made up of males. She has very few friends, even among the female members of our coenobium."

Shortly, the frater in orange appeared. The Mandator ordered him to take the newest noviciator to a vacant cubiculum right there in the bedehouse.

Ranid realized he would be situated adjacent to the apartment of the father and daughter.

⌇

Music from a pneumatic orchestrion filled the evening air with sweet, ethereal notes and melodies. Ranid rose from a small xyloid desk in his room, putting down the Anuran breviarium he had been reading. It was time for vespertine prayers in the oratorium, as he had learned from a lanky brother in orange a little earlier.

All at once, there was a knock at his door. Ranid opened it to find a massive, brawny, athletic person standing there. His square face contained an angular, hooked nose between huge cupreous eyes with a magnetic stare to them.

   CLEMENT S. MASLOFF

"You are the new brother-to-be?" asked the stranger in a bluish red fuchsin robe.

"That is correct," replied the momentarily bewildered newcomer.

"Permit me to introduce myself," grinned the other. "I am the Intendant of this conventiculum, Iwis Nudum. May I welcome you to our spiritual settlement. We are all glad to have you with us. I have spoken to the Mandator about his plans for your education and enlightenment. Are you ready to go to your first vespertine service? We can walk to the fanum together and talk a little along the way."

Ranid soon found himself strolling with this important official of Feretrum along a wide pathway leading to the central building of the walled community. His authority was second only to that of the Mandator, Keigo Tragus. That much was plain to the bewildered novice. It would certainly be beneficial to keep on friendly terms with him, reasoned Ranid.

"I see from your biographical questionnaire that you have studied our system of faith at various sites with different instructors. That is a plus that will help you a great deal. But there is one supreme requirement that is more important than anything else. Without it, knowledge would mean nothing to a person at Feretrum."

"And what could that be, sir?" asked Ranid with an uneasy feeling.

"Perfect obedience," slowly said the Intendant. "Without it, nothing is possible for any candidate to brotherhood with us."

The newly arrived wanderer made no reply, not sure what to say.

Nudum spoke in a mumbling whisper. "I may soon have need for you. A kind of testing of your docility will be given, but only in good time. Do not be surprised when you receive instructions that must be obeyed instantly, without questioning."

The novice said nothing to this, looking ahead to the imposing structure of the fanum.

It was a mammoth stucco building with a testudinate shell as its roof. Verdet green in color, it made Ranid think of a polliwog. Was it given such a shape in order to remind the brothers of a tadpole, the larva of a future frog? he wondered.

The two walkers followed a line of brothers in various colored robes into the oratorium of the great fanum. Iwis Nudum led the new softum to a long bench near the front. The silence was profound and solemn as brothers and sisters filled up all the seating space in the structure.

Ranid made a visual survey of the navis and apsis of the fanum, then the latticed chancel of the Estrada, the stanchions and stringpieces holding up the roof shell, and the spartan collonnettes and columellas along the walls. He had never been in so impressive a templum in his life as a Salamandrite. This was a unique building indeed.

A choir of singers in an upper galleria began a traditional humnoidia dedicated to the sacred frog. At one advanced point, the entire assembly of Anurans joined in. Having memorized the words at the centrum in the swamp country, Ranid was able to add his voice to the rejoicing throng. He felt himself one with the huge congregation.

"Take me to the place where you live,

Let my soul become part of your holy swamp,

Where you live with and unite yourself to

The sacred odyl that grants you its blessing."

When this was finished, there came forward and stood at a pulpitum a brother dressed in a white robe. Ranid surmised that this was the Invocator for the vespertine service. In a high alto voice, he recited from memory a litany of pleas, supplications, and thanksgivings to the elevated spiritual powers, the frog and the odyl it represented. Antiphonal responses arose from the choir. A number of female sopranos were audible among the voices of the brothers, reminding Ranid that the coenobium consisted of persons of both sexes.

When the time came for a discourse by a sermonic, the person who appeared on the pulpitum was no other than Keigo Tragus, the community's Mandator. His powerful baritone rang through the oratorium with bell-like clarity. The lecture was short and edifying, based on the principle of

     CLEMENT S. MASLOFF

truthfulness in all endeavors. His final words made a serious impression on the mind of Ranid.

"Remember, it is your incorporeal soul that decides and shapes the future for you. Just as the invisible odyl animates the great amphibians when we worship them this evening, so your soul and my soul move me and you. That is an eternal, everlasting truth.

"All our souls are mere drops in the sea of being. The endless ocean surrounding us on all sides is the odyle itself, reaching to us through the chosen, supreme creatures, the frogs of our world. We must always remember this blessed connection that the odyl provides for us through the frog. Our peace, happiness, and salvation depend on this amphibian link. It is that which makes life meaningful for us."

As the Mandator left the pulpitum, the entire conventiculum began to sing an old Anuran anthem of devotion: "The true path to blessed odylic energy is known to us, we have it because our predecessors charted it for us..."

When the singing was over, the crowd rose and left the fanum.

Ranid heard a whispered message from the Intendant next to him. "I hope to talk with you tomorrow. Come to my working cubiculum. Anyone can direct you there. Until then, good evening, my new friend."

Chapter XV

Everyone in the fanum repaired to the refectorium hall for the final repast of the day. This consisted of simple avenaceous gruel with barley brewis mixed in it. As Ranid entered the huge eating building, he was surprised by the familiar famulus coming quickly over, as if he had been waiting to see him. The servitor placed a hand on Ranid's lower arm. "The Mandator wishes you to go over and eat at his table. Please follow me."

The stunned softum did as he was told. The tall brother in orange led him to a long table in a secluded alcove of the refectorium. Here was Keigo Tragus at the head of the mensal. On his right was a young woman with red-tinged ginger hair, dressed in a pink and white gown. Obviously, this must be his daughter, thought Ranid. From the corner of his eye, he caught sight of Iwis Nudum, the Intendant. The latter was a few places to the left of the Mandator. Both officials wore long white robes.

"Please sit down here, across from us," warmly invited the Abbad. "One of my people will bring you a bowl of food to eat."

As the novice sat down his eyes met the emerald ones of the small young woman. Exactly the same as her father's, he realized. She had inherited from her father, at least to that extent. There was no doubt about that, she was the Mandator's daughter.

In seconds, a large bowl of gruel was set before him, along with a scooper for him to eat with. Ranid fed himself as Keigo Tragus addressed him.

"Our table usually has fish from local ponds. The small cyprinids and phaxines have a delightful taste to them. I enjoy all our fish, but I have special love for the bogland carpio. And I also demand that our kitchen always have plenty of loach and mudcat. I hope that when they are served in here they will please you, my son.

"Several times each year, on the high holidays of the frog, we indulge ourselves with cisco and lake bloater. When, by good fortune, a donor sends us fish from the Inland Sea, we enjoy whelks, pintado, croakers, and even squeteague. But such delicacies are infrequent, it is sad to say."

All this time, Tragus eyed and studied the softum. He suddenly changed direction.

"I believe you should begin a course of serious reading tomorrow. It will be an intense, demanding exercise. There is much for you to learn about the history and the principles of our precious faith. None of us here in Feretrum has perfect, or even adequate knowledge of all areas of odylogy. The one individual who comes closest to this ideal sits here next to me. I speak of my daughter, Glia. She has devoted her sharp, intelligent mind to thorough, deep study. I receive valuable help from her when I compose my sermons. Yes, her mind possesses amazing retention and agility."

He looked at the small, beautiful young woman, as also did Ranid. She did not appear in any way affected by her father's words of praise, looking at nothing in particular.

The Mandator, after a pause, went on.

"My only difficulty with this philosopher in my family is her speculative audacity. Her thoughts are breathtakingly new and inventive. She constantly creates entirely new structures of ideas that surprise and even startle me. They are very unique. But also difficult to understand, at least for me. For others, as well. I often explain to her that independence of thought is most valuable, but must be tempered by long contemplation, often years of it. My hope is that in time she will see the need for patient reflection and consideration of the new and untried. Our Anuran odylogy is all of one piece, the work of no single individual, but a result of cooperative creation. Any single one of us can add only a tiny morsel to it. Our work must always be joint and united, never too individualistic."

Ranid, his eyes on the daughter, decided to ask her a question.

"What, may I enquire, is the nature of the innovation you conceive of?"

She smiled at him, replying in a high, dulcet tone of honey.

"My father likes to exaggerate, I am afraid. My reading returns me to our earliest Anuran sources, the foundations of the faith. There is no need for anyone to be inventing the new, when so much concerning our beginning and origin remains unexplored. I am attracted to forgotten writings of our early times. That pioneering era has suffered neglect too long. Many documents of that age deserve conscious elucidation. I am especially interested in materials from obscure, secondary locations. They tend to be highly illuminating in many ways."

"Most interesting!" exclaimed Ranid, reminded of his own research at the Archivum in the capital. Instantly, he regretted his show of enthusiasm. What will the others around the mensal think of me? It will be necessary to explain my show of intellectual excitement, he said to himself.

"I have, on my own studied some of the early thinkers and their odylogies," he explained. "Such writings from the faraway past are fascinating. One can never predict what may turn up there. Unexpected ideas are certain to appear. I would like to pursue more such study here at Feretrum if that is possible."

"You must not give up your ambition," insisted Glia with vehemence. Her face looked radiant with an ethereal light. She turned with a shining face to her startled father.

"Perhaps you should assign this softum to a tutular who can instruct him in our early odylogy, Abbad."

The latter gave out a laugh that remained all but soundless.

"That is a splendid suggestion, my dear daughter. Yes, I think I will do that. The idea is brilliant and holds great promise. But the fellow must have someone to guide him through the thicket of spiritual thought. It shall be you, my little philosopher. This moment I appoint you to be the tutular of this new, enthused softum. I can see that he is extremely able. Therefore, I assign him to my most advance thinker, you," he smiled with self-satisfaction.

    CLEMENT S. MASLOFF

The Mandator pursed his mouth as he gazed at the newest resident of Feretrum.

"I thank you, sir," said Ranid to the father, then turned to his daughter. "I thank you, as well."

"Where do you think it best to start?" Glia asked her new pupil. "Is there any particular subject of special interest to your thought?"

Ranid considered only a second. Lowering his voice, he whispered to his new teacher.

"That area of odylogy that, long ago, was termed odylosophy. I hope that it is of interest to you as well. Recent generations have tended to ignore it, but it contains innumerable ideas with deep value."

She grinned at him. "Indeed, it has attracted my interest from my earliest days. There are fascinating subjects in it to consider."

Her student-to-be went on and finished his bowl of gruel, gladdened by his prospects for spiritual advancement in this heart of Anuranism.

Ranid was surprised at the knocking on the door of his cubiculum soon after he rose, a little after dawn the next day.

"Good morning," smiled his appointed teacher. She wore a cerulean vesture that clearly indicated she had a mature woman's form and figure. Her voice had a warm, joyous ring to it. "My father thinks that you should begin to learn and study at once. I have gone to the librarium and collected a number of important rolls and volumes for you to go through. I have them all together in a reading cuddy over there. It is a convenient, comfortable place for you to use."

Her pupil laughed. "That should not take me exceedingly long. In the past, I have had training in fast-reading and become somewhat skilled in that activity."

"That will be of use to you here. But first, let's stop at the refectorium for a speedy breakfast. Then, I can take you to your personal reading sanctum. You will find it a quiet, private place for study and contemplation."

THE AMPHIBIOTS

The exterior of the eating hall glistened with auroral light as the pair approached its entrance. All of a sudden, Ranid spied a familiar towering shape walking into the huge building. He decided to speak about him to his new tutor.

"That is Iwis Nudum, the Intendant. He introduced himself to me yesterday. I was surprised when he said there might in the future be a position for me with him. His words struck me as strange, though. He underlined the need for unquestioning obedience and warned that some sort of testing was coming for me. That was startling and confusing. I still do not know what to make of him. Such a peculiar personage!"

Out of the corner of his eye, Ranid glanced at his companion. He was surprised by the somber frown on her brow. What had affected her so deeply? When she spoke, her voice was hushed up and had an ominous undertone.

"I don't trust that man and am sorry that my father does," she muttered guardedly. "Be careful with him. Should he give you any difficulty, tell me of it. I can get my father to look into the matter."

They entered the refectorium and took an empty mensal in one corner. A server brought them platters of griddlecakes and panada. The two were almost finished eating when Glia started talking again.

"Iwis Nudum is in charge of the pharmaceutic trade that sustains the coenobium of Feretrum. He is the one who oversees the production of medicaments that people travel here for and that we sell outside our walls. The man directs the production of the frog and toad colonies that are the center of our economic activity."

"I take it that you do not value him highly," said Ranid. "What do you accuse this person of? What is his great offense?"

Glia avoided a direct answer by posing her own question.

"Have you ever come across any reference to a group called the Gnomons?" she said out of the blue.

Ranid racked his memory. "That name is mentioned in the early history of the amphibiotic current, before the Great Schism occurred. It was a tiny movement that attempted to establish direct mystical connection with the

        CLEMENT S. MASLOFF

odyle. They were accused by their enemies of trying to bypass intermediary media, whatever they might be. The fear was that they wished to make all amphibians irrelevant. There would be no need for any bridge to the odyl if they succeeded. Each person would be capable of direct contact with the Sublime and Absolute.”

“Our ancestors, the earliest Batrachians, defeated them,” murmured Glia. “But some of those sectaries persisted, hiding underground. They grew mute, pretending not to be mystics. Their movement continues.”

“Continues?” said Ranid in shock.

“There are hints and signs of them here in Feretrum,” she told him in a near whisper.

Chapter XVI

His tutulary presented Ranid a long reading list and several dozen document collections. His first assignment was to formulate and compose in his own words a life of the founder of the Anuran faith. He wrote it with a metallic styloid on a silkpaper roll.

- Scael Imarus, the first Amuran, was an unlikely person to establish a spiritual movement of such an enduring sweep and scope as the one that arose.

- Born in a small delta clachan, his early years were not too different from those of the typical swamplander. The first major turning point in his life came at the age of seventeen, with the winning of a scholarship award to study pharmacology in the capital. This placed him on a path that led to historical greatness. He became closely acquainted with a great variety of substances obtainable from the amphibians, especially the frogs. At a period when Alsike Caldus was roaming about the countryside of Caecilia, Scael was carrying out pioneering research on frog-based remedies for human illnesses. All his time and attention was focused on the life of the frogs. Some of his friends, influenced by the preaching of Alsike Caldus, attempted to recruit the young apothecary into the new movement sweeping the capital, Salamandrism. Scael became adamant in his refusal. He quickly perceived flaws and weaknesses in the radically novel faith. His opposition to it grew intense and personal. Many friendships were lost in spirited arguments over points of odylogy.

- In public debates, Scael tried to refute the principles of salamander superiority. He argued that the wrong amphibian had been selected

CLEMENT S. MASLOFF

to be the primary representative of the Absolute. He began to chart a new, unexpected road of enlightenment. The center of his thought system became the frog. Scael went far beyond ancient Batrachian and Salientian beliefs, unifying the two old faiths into a unified, merged Anuranism that combined toads and frogs into one family of faith.

- Scael promised his followers across Caecilia a new era of prosperity and health if they put their faith in the croaking amphibians. Anuran scientists were expected to make startling discoveries that would transform all of life. Medicinals were now to take a new direction. A corrected and validated doctrine was offered, one based upon rigorous nature study.

- Scael sent missionaries throughout the land, then took to the road himself. He went to war with the ideas of Alsike Caldus and his Salamandrites, drawing many of his followers from their ranks. Conversion was often due to the practical, physical benefits claimed to come from the frog. The Salamandrites soon had a competitor who rivaled them in numbers and fervor. Attempts to conciliate the two sides failed and the Great Schism ensued. Rational Anuranism repudiated Salamandrine obscurantism, in the minds of Scael and his followers.

Glia visited day after day, to accompany him to the refectorium for morning, noon, and evening meals. He completed his first reading assignments with astounding speed. In time he began to delve into new areas and subjects previously not available to him. His eyes moved over pages, not for a single second bored or without curiosity. A sense of what time it was only hit him when Glia would appear at his cubiculum.

"How is it going?" she asked one day at noon. He put down the large folio he had been looking into and gave her an inquiring lock

"Everything I read is fascinating for me. I believe there is enough of value to keep me here for many years to come. My inner spirit has risen to extreme heights. I can hardly believe the progress I have made since beginning."

"Yes, I can see that in your face, Ranid," she said with a friendly laugh.

He rose and followed her out of his reading sanctum.

As the two of them sat eating hackberry flans in the refectorium, a lanky, elderly brother in dark brown workclothes stepped up to their mensal. He addressed Glia in a muffled tone. "Can I have a moment of your time, precious sister?"

The two that were seated looked at him. "What is it, Ereth?" she asked.

"There is a bad situation at the sump. Many dead and poisoned frogs. Could you go and warn your father?"

"Of course. But I think he would like to have a direct report. Could I have a look for myself on what has happened at the sump?"

"That is a good idea, sister," said the one called Ereth. "When shall I see you there?"

Glia thought a moment. "This evening. I can skip vespertine for once."

The old man named Ereth disappeared in a rush. The two at the mensal gazed at each other. Glia decided her pupil had need for an explanation.

"The sump is what we call the frog preserve and reservation. Since the founding of Feretrum, there has existed this special marsh where medicinal varieties of frogs are bred and nursed. For many years, Ereth has been in charge of that entire facility. He is an old comrade of my father. The two have been close to each other since they were children."

"The man now faces some problem with his frogs?" inquired Ranid.

She nodded that he did. "Unexplainable sickness, leading to death. Some sudden plague. I must tell the Mandator and then go to the sump tonight. I am my father's eyes and ears in this matter."

"Could I accompany you, Glia? I know something of amphibian biology."

     CLEMENT S. MASLOFF

The tutulary accepted his offer at once. Thus it came about that Ranid made his first visit to the Feretrum Sump.

The pathway to the concentric structures in the marshland were narrow and circuitous, avoiding the soppiest, spongiest ground. The two walkers, proceeding on in silence, passed by the watergum trees and decayed waterweeds. Shallow ponds and meres were visible in the darkness on both sides of the trail that they treaded.

Ranid, carrying a tiny bull's-eye lantern, lighted the path before them. It threw a ghoulish illumination upon red checkerberries, black thimbleberries, and orange spiceberries that grew in the soil between the water ponds. A pair of phalaropes became frightened by the humans and flew off into the night sky. The two walkers also awoke some water rails, crakes, and ousels. Nasty gallinippes tried to bite at the pair but rarely succeeded.

They came to a low building, from which old Ereth exited at once to meet them. After exchanging greetings, the three stepped into the main cabin of the sump. On a long table, the old man had arranged the dead frogs for the visitors' viewing. The sight was a ghostly one, without question.

"There is no reason or explanation for this," he told the two. "I have never, in all my experience, witnessed anything similar to what you see, and the cause of it is a mystery without solution. This is a biological catastrophe that has never occurred before."

He then guided the pair to a large vitrine tank that held the ill but still alive inhabitants of the swamp preserve. Ranid bent down, looking carefully at each victim of sickness. The frogs had no energy at all. There was an inert quality to every last one of them, without exception.

Glia asked Ereth a question she obviously knew he was unable to answer.

"What can it be? What is causing this strange decline and dying in them?"

No reply came, because none was possible for the caretaker of the frogs.

Soon Ranid and Glia started back homeward to the inhabited center of Feretrum.

"Did you inform the Mandator?" asked Ereth as they left his simple cabin.

"Yes, I did. But he is not feeling well at all. He is spending this evening resting in his cubiculum. I told him to try to sleep. That is the best thing for him at present."

A worried shudder seemed to strike the old man as the pair departed.

Little was said on the way to the residence buildings. The two promised each other to continue with Ranid's training and instruction the next morning. They said good-night and separated.

There was something unexpected for the softum when he opened the door to his cubiculum. A small lantern was burning inside and a huge brother was sitting on a stool.

"Come in, come in," said Iwis Nudum, beckoning him to enter.

Ranid, shaken by his surprise, stepped in and closed the door. He stood an armspan away from the intruder of his personal space.

"You have been to see the devestation at the sump, I understand," began the Intendant. And your young teacher went there with you. Now tell me this: does either of you know what the cause is? What makes them become ill and die?"

Ranid attempted an answer. "It is all a cloudy enigma, it appears. I myself have no idea whatever about the cause of this catastrophe with the frogs. I do not have the slightest notion what may lie this horrible scourge that the unfortunate amphibians happen to be suffering."

CLEMENT S. MASLOFF

Chapter XVII

Nudum made an unusual grimace. "This sudden storm of death is dangerous and menacing to our future supply of medicinals. It must mean something, but what? I, for one, am completely puzzled by it. That is why any idea you have can be of enormous help to me as Intendant. As you know, the Mandator is not feeling well and is confined by the nurser to his cubiculum. The condition of Keigo Tragus is not at all favorable or hopeful. Not at present."

"I didn't know that he was so ill," admitted the softum. "Glia did not describe his illness in any detail to me. I had no idea what he is suffering from."

The Intendant stared with a searching look at Ranid. "We must see each other more often. I believe that you are a novitiate above the average, with sharp perception and a rich imagination. Your instincts tend to guide you in the right direction, more often than not. How do I know this? one may ask. From the shape of your head and the contours of your face. All my life, I have studied and concentrated on human physiology. What can be more important a subject than that? Some look askance at that ancient art, but it can reveal the core of a person's character. Such useful knowledge must not be ignored or scorned. It can help us to make the best decisions in our lives."

Ranid frowned at him. "How, may I ask, do you interpret my hand and face?"

A serious expression covered the countenance of Iwis Nudum as he stared with concentration into the face of the younger man.

"Your physical form is that of a seeker," he said in a whisper. "Curiosity and intelligence shine forth out of your face. You are an individual who craves to know without limit or hindrance. But there is also unacknowledged, unfulfilled ambition hidden deep inside your brain. You are as yet unaware of this. These are the two attributes of your character that I was able to perceive at once, one visible and the other invisible."

Ranid watched the other with amazement. He had never heard anyone talk like that. How should he react to such a strange analysis? He decided on a bold, risky course for himself.

"That is both interesting and exciting. I have always wished to have the ability to read the character of others. If only I could acquire that skill. Must one be born with it, or can that capacity be developed through special training?"

Nudum grinned ecstatically. He had struck the chord he intended to.

"There are physiognomists like me who can teach the principles to selected pupils with the potential to master them."

Ranid forced himself to look excited. "Could I myself learn that arcane art?" he eagerly asked. "Is it at all teachable to others?"

"Certainly," slyly revealed the Intendant. "I have had my eyes on you from the start. My reading of your physiognomy is highly positive. Definitely, you possess possibilities in that sphere, as an interpreter of inner character from the outer form and shape of a person."

"How shall we proceed, then?" asked the softum.

"Your serious studies with the tutulary take up your daytime hours, but we can meet in the early evening, immediately after the vespertine prayers. How would that be for you?"

The Intendant turned and left, leaving Ranid to ponder what other matters he might learn from this odd Amuran, so powerful within Feretrum.

Glia was astounded at the speedy progress that her student made. It was as if he had come to Feretrum fully prepared already for their work together.

　　　　　　　CLEMENT S. MASLOFF

In his private cubby in the librarium, she quizzed him on his reading.

"Tell me what you know of the Anuran concept of the odyle," she asked him.

Ranid recalled sentences he had memorized ahead of time.

"The odyle is known as absolutely bare of any descriptive quality or specific characteristic. Finite beings like us are limited because they possess definable attributes. We have particular limitations. But no limit whatsoever can be predicated of the odyle. To attribute any characteristic to the divine would be to reduce it, to lower it into the realm of finite existences. All we can say of it is that the odyle is infinite, eternal, and unchangeable. It is sufficient unto itself, not dependent on any limited, time-bound being. Of the odyle, we can only say what it is not, not what it is."

He stopped and looked at Glia to see her reaction to what he had stated to her.

"But can we, then, make negative statements about the odyle?" she asked, excited by the strength and clarity of his exposition.

"Some conclusions are possible. But the odyle is the most perfect entity possible. All perfection can be contained within it. The odyle surrounds and encompasses all other things."

"Tell me this: how can the odyle, which is perfect, have connections with the beings of this world of ours, which are all imperfect?"

"Through a medium chosen by the odyle," replied Ranid. "Specifically, the amphibian known as the frog, which serves as its instrumentality in our world."

"Why cannot human beings have immediate contact with the odyle?"

He remembered what the Intendant had promised to teach him, but set it aside for the time being as not relevant to this question.

"The absolute perfection, purity, and loftiness would be defiled and violated by touching directly the imperfect, impure, and finite creatures of this fallen world. Only through the mediation of the frog can there be any tie between the odyle and the cosmos. The former remains eternally without quality, but it can speak and act through its chosen creatures. Only through them can we know or reach to the divine."

His teacher smiled with satisfaction and joy.

"You are an excellent learner, Ranid. I have never seen anyone master the principles of odylogy as fast as you have. But the search for truth involves much more than placing ideas together into a formal system. Do you have the desire to go much further on your own? I can assist you if that is true. You will become a dedicated seeker and searcher, I believe."

For a moment, the softum battled for his breath.

"Yes," he finally grinned in victory. "That is what I came here for. To hunt for the deepest truth I could find. To learn what it is and allow it to enter into my life. That is my highest, most cherished goal in life."

Glia looked him directly in the eye.

"I hoped you would answer that way, Ranid. I have taken an original, individual path on my own, too. Many here in Feretrum consider my ideas unorthodox and heretical. I have had to write my ideas down in secret. Even my father knows nothing of them. He has never read my short treatise on the hypostasis of the odyle. I have kept close watch over its privacy. No one has broken into my private realm of advancing thoughts. I have organized my reflections and speculations around the concept of the hypostasis."

"I have come across that term in my reading but don't at all understand it," admitted Ranid. "What exactly is the meaning of hypostasis? How is it connected to the odyle? Can you explain it to me?"

"It would be best for you to read my essay first. Then, you can ask specific questions about the matter."

"Good," beamed the student. "I will study your personal writing with the attention it deserves."

What am I now involved in? wondered the spiritual explorer who had only recently arrived in Feretrum.

　　　CLEMENT S. MASLOFF

Two developments alarmed the inhabitants of the coenobium: the illness of their Mandator and the sudden demise of so many sump frogs. Ranid could read the worry and concern of Glia in her face and eyes. He felt helpless to relieve her trauma. What could he do?

Perhaps there was something he could learn from Nudum, the Intendant. But what might that be? He decided to go along with the man who now, in effect, ran the coenobium of Feretrum. But why was it that this frater made him so uneasy? he asked himself.

Another series of questions also bothered him. What is the Intendant after? Why is he in pursuit of associating with me? It was clear to Ranid that the official was trying to recruit him into some kind of ambitious enterprise. What could it be? What was its end purpose?

What ambitious plan did Iwis Nudum have in mind? wondered the new resident in Feretrum.

Chapter XVIII

Ranid was pondering the problems facing him when Glia returned with her secret treatise. He sensed some frenetic emotion in her. It had to be connected to the illness of her father.

"How is the Mandator today?" he asked with sympathy.

Her face seemed to turn into stone. "Worse and worse every day, every hour. I can't understand it. No one has ever seen anything like it before."

He took her handwritten monograph and placed it on the console table, planning to spend the entire afternoon studying it in detail.

The sad-faced tutulary departed without another word to her pupil.

Ranid became enthralled with the revelatory sentences in the essay written by his new teacher, Glia Tragus.

"The odyle is the hub of universal unity. Thus, it must be immanate in each and every part of the whole. The odyle is a predicateless odylehead. It is unknowable directly by mankind. Its essence holds the potentiality of all existing things everywhere through time.

"The odyle has many stages it goes through in an eternal self-revealing process. This continual revelation is never ended. The eternal creation of the world reflects the eternal self-generation of the original odyle.

"The dark and formless essence of the odyle is its odylehead. The latter resembles an abyss, an eternal nothing, a hidden place without any essence. It merely is, but it is no specific, individual being.

"The medium called the anuran frog is an emanation out of the odyle. But since the odyle is not directly known or perceived, it must have an aziluth.

"What is the aziluth? It is like a single ray from the luminary called the daystar. The aziluth is incomprehensible because of its infinitude. It is a reflection of the intentional activity of the odyle in itself.

"The odyle has an inner desire to be known. Therefore, the desire to create has always been co-eternal with it. The aziluth is in perpetual unity with the odyle. It is necessary for the completeness of the odylehead itself. It is never external to the odyle or ever enjoys access to it from without. Its contact with the odyle cannot be broken.

"The natural daystar in the sky is a representation of the spiritual daystar of the odyle. This divine orb is the source of all life, all love, and all intelligence. The purposeful end of all creation has from the beginning been the conjunction of the rational sphere with the spiritual sphere.

"The aim and destination of all creation is the Final Unity.

"Each person's soul must turn into a medium of the odyle, an instrumental agent of the Absolute and the Sublime. Every anuran soul must transcend the sacred frog and conjoin itself to the divine odylehead by finding the aziluth within itself."

Ranid took a rest from reading the essay, breathing hard. His mind was in a state of whirling wonder. The thoughts of Glia seemed to him like an echo of thoughts he had previously come across somewhere. Whose were they? Why did these ideas seem familiar to him?

He was suddenly reminded of what he carried with him in the secret diary of Alsike Caldus, founder of the Salamandrine faith. Was there some similarity there? An unconscious resemblance between the two varieties of thought? Could that be possible?

"The Original Being we call the odyle throws out the aziluth with a perfect image within itself. This is the image of the One, the Archtype of all existing entities. The aziluth, therefore, is composed of both thought and being. The odyle is perpetually producing something else without diminution or alteration of itself. All this creation occurs through and by the aziluth.

"As a reflected image, the aziluth corresponds perfectly to the One odylehead. But as a derivative from it, the aziluth is completely separate and different. The aziluth is the highest sphere accessible to the human mind on its own.

"The reflection of the aziluth is found in the soul. The latter's relationship to the aziluth is identical to that of the aziluth to the One, the odylehead.

"Since the aziluth is indivisible, the soul can only preserve its unity by contact with it. The path to the odyle lies there. If the human soul unites itself only with the corporeal world, it eventually disintegrates. The alternative to union with the aziluth and therefore the odyle is to sink into the sensual, to become lost in the finite. This brings about a final ruin.

"Material lust traps most souls. Individuals lose themselves in a false existence.

"Only freedom from material sensuality can lead a person back to the original self.

"An ascetic life allows one to contemplate the primal odyle through the azimuth.

"One must become bathed in the Light of Eternity, swallowed up in the highest ecstatic bliss. A person has to become free of the tyranny of circumstances and live in the freedom of the eternal elements of being."

Ranid felt a perceptible shudder down his back.

Was Glia veering close to the mysticism of the Gnomens? he asked himself with trepidation.

Iwis Nudum arrived as expected that evening. He quietly slipped into the cubiculum with a scroll in the pocket of his robe, drawing it out and handing it to the young man sitting at the desk.

 CLEMENT S. MASLOFF

"These drawings will help you identify cardinal physical traits that indicate particular types of characters, my good fellow."

The softum opened the scroll and saw numerous drawings of faces. Iwis, standing behind him, pointed out facial traits and described what each one meant for analysis of personality.

"A sharp nose indicates the person is easily provoked to anger, like a dog. But a round, large nose points to an individual who is peaceable and magnanimous, like a lion. A slender, hooked nose belongs to an eagle-like person, searching and very painstaking. When a nose is round-tipped it reflects laziness and luxuriousness. A slight notch at the root of a nose reveals that one is quarrelsome, even impudent, like a crow. A snub nose belongs to a person of artistic temperament, one with a fanciful imagination. And open nostrils are a sign of romantic passion.

"I wish you to study all of these drawings, Ranid, so that you immediately recognize what the character of each classification is. Will you do so tonight? This is much more important than the assigned readings given you by the daughter of the Mandator. What I will provide has practical application every day, unlike her empty generalities."

The softum nodded his head. "I will make myself time to read this scroll," he promised.

"You must give it priority. Not every novitiate is granted such special knowledge. Only someone like you who possesses the proper physiognomy is able to. Do you understand me?"

"Only a limited few enjoy access to these secrets," muttered Ranid. "This knowledge, then, is abstruse and recondite. Is there a secret name for those who master this arcane subject?"

Iwis furrowed his forehead. The cupreous eyes glowed and grew large.

"Have you ever heard the word gnomen, my son?"

"No," pretended Ranid. "I haven't. It is foreign to me."

The Intendant leaned forward, his voice falling until it was nearly inaudible.

"We are only a small circle here at Feretrum, yet we have the secret of immediate union."

"Union?" questioned the softum sitting at the desk.

"With the odyle itself. Without any imtermediary or instrumentality."

A tense silence ensued.

"What about the frog?" asked Ranid, slowly and softly.

"When you have joined us and learned our methods, you can then place any creature in its proper place. By then, there will be no need to depend on any medium at all. At that point, you are more than an isolated gnomen. Much more, much more. You become an exalted energumen, possessed by the odyle itself. That is a sublime, exalted state of being. It is the ultimate, highest step a human being is capable of."

Ranid could hardly believe what he had just heard.

"I want to learn all that I can, as quickly as possible." he said with feverish enthusiasm. "When can you begin to teach me how to find...union?"

"Enosis, that is the old technical term. Mystical enosis with the invisible odyle that created all things. That is the final aim."

"There is much for me to learn first, I take it," said the pupil.

"Physiognomy is a simple method of understanding other souls," explained the Intendant. "We must start there, then proceed to the deeper areas, and finally to full union."

Ranid did not try to conceal the excitement he felt over what he had just heard said.

"Every gnomen is able to read and understand souls, then?"

"Do you think that thoughts can be concealed within our inner reaches?" returned Iwis. "Of course not, when one focuses on all that rises out of the intimate thoughts of the swamp people."

The softum smiled kindly. My own soul does not appear to be understandable, he thought to himself.

 CLEMENT S. MASLOFF

"I want you to study and memorize these face drawings," said Nudum. "I will see you tomorrow night. We will investigate how swiftly progress is being made by you."

Chapter IXX

Ranid now found himself on two opposite tracks. Sporadically, he studied the scroll of the gnomons. But most of the night and day were spent on the difficult secret essay of Glia Tragus.

Each day in the librarium sanctum, he asked her scores of questions.

"What is the concrete meaning of hypostasis?"

"Its root has the sense of a base, a foundation. The underlying substance or essence of an entity. In other words, its central principle."

"But how does all this pertain to the odyle and its medium, the frog?"

Glia answered him slowly and patiently.

"The odyle is the creative force, the spermatic power that produced everything in the universe. Within every existent being, therefore, there is this subsistent floor, this foundation. We can think of this as the hypostasis of the odyle, but it is inside every separate particle of our world. And the hypostasis of each and every individual entity is also inside the odyle, as an idea or a thought component."

The softum persisted questioning. "Then, all of the created cosmos contains something of the original being, the odyle. That must be so, according to what you conclude in your treatise. That is how I understand the situation."

Cautiously, the tutulary nodded. "What are you getting at?" she demanded.

CLEMENT S. MASLOFF

"Why is the medium of the odyle defined so narrowly, when everything partakes of the same hypostasis? Why define it so exclusively, when one and all are interconnected as if by strings?"

Glia looked shocked. "Narrowly, you say?"

"Why can't any being become a medium? Specifically, why are all amphibians except the frog excluded from primacy in the Anuran system?"

She seemed to turn pale.

"There are historical reasons, for one thing. We live in a country of swamps and marshes where one amphibian is often considered supreme. What you are saying might be used by a Salamandrite to elevate the salamander and negate the frog's importance."

The pair stared at each other without speaking. All at once, Glia changed the subject.

"I forgot to tell you that my father is feeling even worse. His pain is excruciating. No one can say when the illness will turn around. And it is only a short while until the Encaenia, our greatest holiday at Feretrum. He says that he must be up and about when the throngs of outside visitors come for our celebration. But how can he recuperate so fast?"

"Has there been any determination on what the illness is?" asked Ranid with concern.

She shook her head. "No, there is no way to be certain. He is receiving several medicaments from our hygeist, Brother Omphal."

"I have never met such an individual. It would please me to speak with him. Do you think I could make a short visit to your father when this healer happens to be present? That way I can become acquainted with the man."

She thought a second. "I can take you this very moment. Come along, Ranid."

The two of them departed from the librarium, the young woman leading the way.

The Mandator lay motionless on a straw pallaisse, under a pale yellow sheet. His face possessed a flavescent gauntness. The once plump figure had dropped much of its weight. Desperation and despair dimmed his eyes of emerald. They no longer had the luster of gems. The voice he spoke with was dry and weak.

"Thank you for coming to see me," whispered Keigo Tragus, letting go of the hand of the softum after holding it tightly. "My daughter says that you are making large strides forward in your studies. I am pleased to hear that. You are on the road to genuine enlightenment."

"I have the best instructors, sir," smiled Ranid, not looking directly or indirectly at Glia, though sensing her body to his side. "But there is still much more for me to absorb. I am only a beginner in odylogy. I have so much further to go."

The Mandator suddenly fell into a state of reverie and reminiscence.

"I remember how it was for me when I first arrived here. Do you know who it was that made me come to Feretrum? It was my wife, Glia. My daughter was named for her mother, a fervent believer in the frog. She convinced me to enroll as a novitiate, along with her. We worked and studied together. Her help was indispensable. She, in the most profound sense, made me what I am. But now..."

He halted, his face suffering a severe spasm of pain. Glia stepped forward to the side of the paillasse and placed a hand on his temple.

"Your fever is back, father. Rest and quiet is what you need at this time. We will leave and let you fall asleep again. That is what you need at this moment."

"I can't sleep any way, Glia," the sick man murmured. "This torment comes and goes by itself, and I can't do anything to stop it. Nothing at all."

"Where was I?"

His emerald eyes found Ranid and held him in sight.

"My wife, she was the cornerstone of everything I achieved. It was for her that I delved into my studies. Never did I have any idea of rising in rank.

     CLEMENT S. MASLOFF

But growing responsibilities were given to me. I began at the Frog Sump. The lowest of labor was assigned to me. That was where I first became a manager and then a leader." He thought of something and quickly turned to Glia.

"How are the frogs now? Has any change occurred there?"

"It is the same as before," replied his daughter. "A few more die each day."

Keigo's face became an expressionless mask over his inner ruminations.

"Something must be causing this," he said darkly. "But what can it be?"

All of a sudden, an inspiration arose in the mind of Ranid.

"Sir, could I request something of you?"

The Mandator turned his head toward him. "What is it?" he inquired.

"Although I am still only a softum, there is no reason why a work task cannot be assigned to me. Therefore, I ask that you send me to the Sump. I have already met Ereth, who would supervise me. We appear to get along with each other. I would work under him, assisting in whatever he chooses. Would such an arrangement be possible?"

"Certainly," replied the ailing sufferer. "Why not? If that is what you desire, I shall grant you permission to join with Ereth at the Sump."

So it came about that Ranid was granted access to the highly distressed facility where frogs were bred for medicinal purposes.

-

As Glia and the softum made their way out of her father's bed-cube, a lanky man with inky hair and eyes to match approached the two.

"I'm glad I found you, Glia," said the tall, skinny figure. "We must talk about your father and his deteriorating condition."

This is the hygeist treating the Mandator, surmised Ranid to himself. That became clear when the young woman introduced the two men to each other. Neither offered a hand to the other.

"You can speak before the two of us," indicated Glia to the coenobium's medical healer. "Has your prognosis changed in any way? Has any improvement at all occurred?"

Omphal replied to this in a subdued, cautious manner.

"His cycle of pain and temporary relief spins on, each time dropping to a lower level than before. Much damage has already occurred to the organs. Nothing has been able to halt the regression of his health, despite the many palliatives I have tried."

He stopped, looking into the daughter's face with desperation. When he began to speak again, his voice was low and hollow.

"Serious intrusion into his body may soon become necessary. I foresee the need to perform organic chirurgery within his interior areas. Even now, that appears to be inevitable. There is no way I know to avoid the necessary surgery."

For several moments there was silence. But then Glia asked an important question of the medico.

"Are we at that point yet? Do such serious measures have to be taken before too long?"

"The critical moment is quite near, I am afraid," replied Omphal, his eyes downcast now. "I will not conceal from you the high degree of risk involved should surgical intervention be left as the last, final alternative. Perhaps I have already waited too long. That is always a real possibility. Your father's condition is a very serious one. It is approaching the point of becoming critical."

The medical hygeist went into the bed-cube by himself.

Ranid took leave of Glia, saying that he was going at once to the Frog Sump to discuss his new duties there with Ereth.

CLEMENT S. MASLOFF

Chapter XX

Ranid and Ereth became better acquainted. They discussed frog life and illnesses at length, and went into their sensitivity to foreign substances. Ranid announced that he wished to survey all past records and documents at the Sump. He sensed a great love for the frogs in Ereth. It became more evident with each day that passed.

Ranid returned each evening to his sleeping cube at the center of Feretrum. It was Nudum who knocked and came in to see him late one night, causing surprise and alarm to the occupant.

Iwis handed the softum a small, tattered folio.

"You must read through this tonight, while we are here together. I cannot allow this material to be out of my custody, not for a second. So, I shall wait until you finish it. Then, I will reclaim and leave with it. Is that understood? Do you agree to the terms I have set for you, my friend?"

Ranid nodded that he would comply, then opened the folio and hurried through its startlingly scandalous pages. Everything he read was a shock to him. He had never thought he would see such words on a page.

- Anuranism has become dogmatic and ossified. The odyle has been turned into an object external to the world. It is far away and foreign to us. In truth, it could grant us miraculous personal experiences if we called upon it. A new supreme soul is needed for all of us: a direct union with the odyle itself. The human soul within each of us is a mirror reflection of the odyle. Its image is already there within each of us, but covered and unseen. It is waiting to become visible to us. That image must be liberated and allowed to develop.

- The soul is a stranger within this world. There is an inner instinct in everyone to repudiate the senses and the sensible. Material existence is estrangement from the infinite, eternal odyle. We should be ashamed of being inside a body. What the soul seeks and needs is a uniting into the odyle. One must melt and fuse with it. Even thought and thinking must be left behind. Thought is only a form of motion, nothing else. We have to seek and reach beyond it for the motionless rest that belongs to the odyle alone.

- The odyle created the visible world. It preceded the cosmos, and is its universal soul. The world is inside that all-embracing soul, not the other way around. This world reflects what has always been yonder in the odyle. Everything outside it is secondary.

- The odyle is the nameless One. The consummation of all living is to return to it. One must transfuse oneself through transcendental union. Inner vision will result in coalescence and supreme ecstasy. One must then dissolve into the Ineffable, the Unspeakable. Purification and enlightenment will result in spiritual unification. This is a process called odylesis. One becomes united with the odyle. A person moves oneself into the divine and fuses with the latter.

- The Gnomen knows how to ascend beyond the self, into Enosis with the odyle. At first, there is the experience of darkness, nakedness, and nothingness. But beyond knowledge and existence a final unity is revealed as if in a phantasmal trance. The individual soul will take on a new form. Odyllic power radiates it. This is a path of self-negation, dropping every definite attribute, characteristic, and determinant. The soul becomes free at last, free in a Union. One is, at last, home.

Ranid finished reading, folded the folio, and handed it back to Nudum, who was perched on a low cricket stool.

"I see nothing in this about the frog as a medium. Isn't it needed, then?"

The Intendant appeared to smirk. "Whatever is not needed must fall into a limbo of oblivion. Does that not seem reasonable to you, my son?"

　　　CLEMENT S. MASLOFF

A direct question was necessary from himself, decided the softum. "How did you come to join a group of such mystagogues as the Gnomens, sir?"

All at once, Nudum flushed red with anger. "I don't see how that pertains to you, but it will do no harm to tell you the story. Upon first coming to Feretrum, my assignment was to carry out manual labor in the Frog Swamp. It was there that I first heard this, to me, strange doctrine. A small group of swampmen initiated me into the mysteries. In truth, it was in the home of the real frogs that I learned of the true path to spiritual enlightenment." He suddenly remembered something important. "It has come to me that you have been assigned to work under Ereth at the Sump. I can tell you this: he himself is not one of us, but serves as the center of the circle of the Gnomens. They would be lost without his exact knowledge of the frogs. He is important and vital to their successful operations and activities."

A sudden inspiration entered the mind of Ranid. "If I knew a name or two, I could converse and get to know them."

Iwis had no need to think long about this. What better way was there to draw the softum into the small, concealed sect?

"There is one you should especially ask to see. He is a kind of leader at the Sump, and his name is Atpl. Yes, he is Atpl Nudum and we share the same surname. We happen to be distant consanguines. He is my remote relative and a close associate of mine."

"I will meet with that man," promised Ranid, hoping to learn from that source about the Gnomens and their goals. For he nursed a deep suspicion of the Intendant and anyone who might be associated with him. The new softum neither liked nor trusted this person who held the finances of Feretrum in his hands.

Nudum took the folio, placed it into his sleeve pocket, and left the cubiculum.

Ranid considered and weighed his options for a time, then made a major decision. It was not worthy of him to keep so much from Glia. The time had come for complete disclosure of his venture into gnomenic mysticism. This was the moment for revealing what he had been silent about with her till now. And tomorrow he would go to the Frog Sump to get acquainted with a promising Gnomen source.

Ereth vigorously shook hands with his newest worker, Ranid Rolius.

"Your job will be the one that my entire crew is involved in day and night: gathering up the corpses and the afflicted living frog residents. There is nothing more we can do beyond to pick up and dispose of the ones that have died or will die soon. We possess no compound that can save them. And I don't even know what it is that kills so many frogs. It is a horrible situation for all of us."

"There is nothing similar to this described in the historical records of your office?" asked Ranid.

Erath shook his head in grief at his helplessness. Then he instructed the new frog sump worker further in his tasks and responsibilities.

"You will be locating and picking up victims around the ponds," said the older man. "My crew works in pairs, so that no one has to act on their own. They place the corpses in special scuttles we use to transport frogs from place to place. Let's see, the person who will show you how it is best done is the man in charge of the outdoor crews. He should be coming in here soon. His name is Atpl Nudum."

The new worker swallowed hard. Things seemed to be going his way, for the time being.

This relative of the Intendant did not resemble him in the slightest degree. He was small, wiry, and mouse-like, looking completely unsuited to any work in the Frog Sump.

As Ranid shook his hand, he concluded that he was stationed here as the eyes and ears of his nepotal. It would be necessary to treat him with great caution.

"Do you have any experience in swamp work?" gruffly asked the man named Atpl.

 CLEMENT S. MASLOFF

"No, none at all. I will have to learn everything from the ground up," said Ranid, implying that he needed thorough instruction in the basics of his job.

The crew chief gave him a look of scorn. "When you've been here for twenty years, like I have, you'll know every one of the jobs in the Sump. But first, I'll have to get you a scuttle and show you the best way to pick up dead frogs."

Atpl went to a small nearby shed and took out two shallow metallic scuttles. "This is what we put the frogs in, so they can be carried back to the main cabin. There is a lot of bending of the back involved, but it has to be done. Nobody wants corpses stinking up the ponds."

"What were your primary duties before this terrible plague hit the frogs?"

Atpl handed one scuttle to Ranid.

"From the first, I was put in charge of gallinipper protection. They taught me that twenty years ago. My teachers have passed away, so I'm the one now in charge of insect control. I have always specialized on mosquitoes."

Ranid looked puzzled. "Why should that be necessary here in the open air outdoors? I don't understand what needs protection and control."

The other man seemed to be getting angry. "It's not your business, for now. All that is my responsibility alone. Right now, let's start looking for dead or sick frogs. That's the job we have to perform at this moment."

Chapter XXI

Glia met him in the antechamber of the Mandator's apartment. It was late evening, and she was surprised to see him at that hour. He was first to speak.

"Your father, has there been any change in him?"

"No," she said with a moan. "He seems to be sinking at the same rate as when you yourself saw him. I fear leaving him to get sleep. Who can say how he will be next morning? And the pain never seems to leave him, not for a second. It is an awful scene for me to be seeing. I never expected anything like what is happening to him now."

"Glia, tomorrow I shall start work at the Frog Sump. There will be little time now for study in the librarium. But there is a matter that I have hesitated to tell you about. Now I have decided, this is the right time for me to relate this to you."

She looked puzzled. "What are you talking about, Ranid?"

He swiftly disclosed the history of his meetings with Nudus and how the Intendant tried to convert and recruit him into the bizarre mystical sect of the Gnomenists.

Glia's mouth opened and her pupils dilated. As he continued, disbelief turned to belief. When he had finished, she was full of questions. As best he could, Ranid answered them point-by-point. He was able, from memory, to give her the content of the folio given him to read by the Intendant.

"He learned these heretical theories while a worker at the Frog Sump?"

     CLEMENT S. MASLOFF

"That's what he claims," replied the softum. "And there still remains a small coterie of his comrades there. I plan to investigate among them. I asked for a name to look for and Nudus told me who the primary Gnomen is there. It will be necessary for me to acquaint myself with him. I suspect there is a hidden conspiracy involved in the frog decimation. I want to prove it and locate the links to the Intendant himself. He is behind all of this. That is certain."

She wrinkled the skin of her brows. "Do you remember when I warned you about him? Years ago, when I was in my early teens, he frightened me terribly. I never told anyone, not even my father. But that is why I came to loath the man."

She ended with a nervous shudder. It seemed to seize control of her whole body. When it was over, she spoke once again. "He grabbed me around my breast and tried to feel and squeeze, but I stiffened and pushed back. My resistance made him release me." She looked away, to one side.

As he heard this, Ranid grew angry and excited. He extended his right arm, taking her left hand and holding it tightly.

"I would have protected you, Glia, then or afterwards, or at any time at all. What you say crushes me inside. If only I could have shielded you!"

She made a wry smile. "You were elsewhere then. And no physical assault was allowed to occur. But I never forgot what a hypocritical rogue he is beneath his outer mask. I was never able to describe the incident to my father. As the years passed, it became too late for that. And he stayed away from me, or at least seemed to do so. But we rarely ever exchanged a word between us."

The two of them fell silent, both of them unable to proceed any further or deeper.

"I intend to find out if there is a subterranean conspiracy at Feretrum," he promised. "Keep up your spirits, Glia. There may come a turnabout for your father's condition."

With that said, he let go of her hand and walked out of the antechamber.

Ereth was troubled and exhausted, collecting and examining dead frogs without end or intermission. There seemed to be nothing he could do about the doomed amphibians that had come down with the unknown fatal disease. He led Ranid around the tables where the inert bodies lay.

"It will be a mighty help to me having you here at the Sump. Your task will be to assist in the disposal of the dead frogs."

All that morning, Ranid refrained from asking any more questions of the touchy nepotal. But during the noontime rest, he went to the central cabin to see what he could learn about insect control from the friendly, trustworthy sumpman, Ereth.

"How did your first tour of the ponds go?" asked the latter.

"Not bad at all," replied the softum. "One fact struck me: I saw very few gallinippers around. But Atpl mentioned that he is in charge of keeping their population down. That struck me as hard to believe or rationalize. What possible danger could there be from them? They bite, of course. But why take them so seriously? Why so much fright?"

Ereth grinned for a moment. "I asked that same question when I first came here. They told me that it was a custom established by the founders of Feretrum. The actual reason had long been forgotten. But the original objective, I learned, was to prevent and avoid paludal fever in the members of the coenobium. That disease was stamped out way back then, but the tradition of killing off its carriers continued. We still put out the toxicants even today."

"Interesting," was all that Ranid said at this point, soon leaving to begin collecting corpses on his own, without pressures from the nepotal.

When Ranid returned to the center of Feretrum that evening he did not go to the vespertine service in the fanum, but instead crept into the librarium. There was a particular subject that he had to look up. Was there anything recorded about gallinippers and the danger of some sort of paludal fever?

 CLEMENT S. MASLOFF

Already, many preparations were finished for tomorrow's Day of Encaenia. He could see wreaths and decorations marking the anniversary of the establishment of the community of Feretrum. The holiday and the festival would soon be upon all of them. Ranid suddenly thought of Glia and her stricken father. What would those two possibly have to celebrate?

Ranid had no success at first. Nothing connected to the Frog Sump mentioned the gallinipper as a health threat. On and on the reader went, his fish-oil lamp burning low again and again. Not a word could be found about what he wanted to know. The night went on, until he was the lone individual left in the building.

I must see Glia in the morning, he told himself.

There was something that happened at the time of the foundation of the coenobium. What could it have been? He began to browse about at random in the old folios and scrolls. If he only knew what it was he was hunting for! Something about galliippers and paludal fever.

Then he stumbled onto an oblique reference with significance for him. It was a short, hazy note about a distant, forgotten incident.

"In the third year after the establishment of Feretrum, when the Frog Sump was being formed, an old group of vagabonds arrived. They were hungry and were given food. Their claim was to being swampmen seeking employment. We asked whether they had experience with the care of frogs and their answer was yes. But they worked only three weeks at digging and hauling soil before their secret was uncovered. At the time, the wanderers said they had to rid the sump of culicines and anephelines. Their leader said that he possessed a special mosquito bane that had the power to get rid of them. Its name was ceratophrys, a strange unfamiliar term for everyone outside their small group of tramps. Before they began to apply this unknown bane, though, all of these men were exposed as Gnomens and expelled at once from Feretrum."

Ranid drew breath into his lungs with an extremely deep gasp.

Had he discovered the key with which to unlock this mysterious amphibian tragedy?

It was past midnight, yet he found Glia still awake when he rapped on the door of her cubiculum. Should he inform her of what he had found out about the Frog Sump? It was better to wait and present her with a full story, he decided. There would surely be time enough for disclosure later. Why rush into such a disturbing subject as that?

"Your father?" he asked her. "How is he?"

"Unconscious, in deep coma," she moaned. "No one knows when he will awaken again."

"Tomorrow begins the Encaenia, but he will not be part of it, will he?"

"No, that is impossible. That will give the Intendant the official duty of presiding at all the many ceremonies. I am certain he will enjoy himself and take the opportunity to widen his power and position."

"It's a shame, a scandal," grumbled Ranid. "This man was born without any conscience. Feretrum would be completely changed if he should become the dominant official here."

All of a sudden, the softum moved closer to his tutulary. What he did next was unforeseeable and unplanned. The kiss that was given was a light, delicate buss on the middle of her forehead. There were no words and no embracing. Nothing but the brotherly peck, gentle and nonaggressive. But sufficient to communicate what he was feeling about her.

Without any more words, Ranid departed.

Returning to his cube, the tired novitiate was eager for sleep. But before he could lie down and rest, he had a dreaded visitor, the Intendant.

How much did Nudum know about today's and tonight's activities? It was necessary to speak with heightened care and caution. Nothing was to be told to this evil-minded Gnomen, a corrupt and depraved mystic who only considered himself and his own selfish interest. His ignorance was to be preserved.

"How did your first day of work go?"

Ranid tried to look indifferent. "Not badly. It wasn't as hard as I imagined."

"You met my nepotal, Aptl Nudum?"

"Yes, we worked together in the morning. He taught me the requirements of my task."

"I see," muttered the other. "Tell me, what do you think of him?"

"I don't know, but he seemed an ordinary brother. There was nothing too odd or different about him. He seemed to be quite normal. That was the impression that he made upon me, I believe."

Ranid was aiming at giving an answer with no untoward implications in it, that meant and implied very little at all.

"He is a Gnomen, but not too effective at it. Ties of family mostly brought him into our group. I believe that when you become a full member of our circle, you can take over as the crew chief out there. He can be a good second to you. That would be the best of arrangements, I think."

"You are saying that I can replace your relative?" said Ranid with surprise.

A knowing smile crossed the face of the Intendant.

"When Aptl is brought into a job here alongside me, you can be of enormous value to us at the Sump." Since Ranid made no response, Nudum continued. "There will be changes in the coenobium, and they are not too far in the future. Once they happen, you will be told what you are to do. Until then, be ready for immediate orders. They may come up very soon. You should be ready to receive and carry them out."

This was puzzling to the softum. Was the Intendant referring to a hidden conspiracy to take over command of Feretrum? It might appear to be so, if one were to leap to a sudden surmise. Was a seizure by force planned? What method did the Intendant plan to use?

"You shall not be here for the celebration tomorrow," went on Nudum. "Stay close to my nepotal and do whatever he orders you to. Understand?"

Ranid nodded that he did, though in truth his confusion had become complete.

He was most happy when the visitor turned around and left.

After only an hour or so of genuine sleep, he slipped off for the Frog Sump an hour or so before dawn.

Scores, then hundreds and several thousand Anurans flocked to Feretrum as the morning passed. The mood of these pilgrims was a festive one, regardless of the troubles at the Frog Sump. They were present to commemorate the founding of this spiritual community, but also the glories of the frog-based faith. The travelers from far and wide were determined to have themselves a good time. On the main meadow, mensals were set up for games of spoilfive, scarto, and slapjack, run by the brothers. Outsiders were present to engage in a variety of other sporting activities with cards: canfield, lansquenet, cooncan, conquian, videruff, gleek, slam, primero, piquet, cinch, pedro, muggings, and monte.

Games of chance, luck, and skill were available for every kind of taste, every degree of risk.

At small stalls, women sold cracknels, maypops, soursops, sweetsops, shandygaff, and farl cakes. Homemade oenomel was being drunk on all sides, by nearly everyone. Visitors ate baked fish from nearby streams, enjoying the taste of tench and mudcat. Festive emotions prevailed, catching hold of everyone like a spreading infection.

The crowd in the coenobium's meadow grew constantly larger and noisier. Kettles of hot posset rapidly turned empty as drinkers poured the milky wine into their mouths and down their throats. Eager thirsts remained unsatisfied. The music of a theorbo band raised the spirits of the many jolly revelers. Sudden, unexpected dancing broke out at numerous locations, again and again.

Young men in short curtails played at tip cat, knocking wooden pieces into the air with strength and abandon. Costermongers sold nugae of every conceivable kind to the crowd of visitors from outside.

     CLEMENT S. MASLOFF

At the far end of the meadow, pantominists in frog-green costumes enacted ancient Batrachian legends. Spectators surrounded them on all sides. A furtive chiromancer tried to read palms and tell fortunes in a quiet, secluded grove, away from onlookers, keeping away from the squads of brothers who kept the peace and order of the Encaenia.

The thousands of celebrants looked forward to noontime, when the highest magistral of Anuranism was expected to arrive and officiate over the day's cult services and ceremonies.

Ranid conversed with Ereth for several hours, explaining his findings in the librarium. Neither one of them had reached any solid, final conclusions about what the Gnomens were up to at the Frog Sump. What was the ceratophrys that was considered in many sources to be a hazardous bane? What was its true nature, and how important was it?

"There is one person who can give us answers," muttered Ereth, sitting at the eating mensal in the central cabin. "We have to interrogate Aptl at once. There is no other way. I would like to have you go and tell him I want to discuss a certain matter with him."

This mission took only a minute for the softum to fulfill. He returned with the nepotal and followed him back into the cabin where Ereth waited.

How were they going to break the expected resistance of this relative of the Intendant? Suddenly, a way to outwit this man with special knowledge struck the mind of Ranid. What if they pretended to be part of the Gromen movement themselves? Was such a deception at all possible?

Ranid had to seize the reins before Ereth began to question the swampman.

"What is the ceratophrys, brother? The Intendant told us to get it from you, so that it can be used for a new, unprecedented purpose of importance."

Aptl spun around, facing Ranid and giving him a confused, uncertain look.

"You are one of us? And so is he?"

He turned around to gaze at the equally surprised manager of the Frog Sump.

Erath stared back at Aptl in silence, sensing that Ranid was carrying out some delicate, intricate strategy.

The nepotal started to speak directly to the new softum.

"Are you a Gnomen, then? How can that be? Why wasn't I told of it?"

Ranid decided to play by ear and see what would happen.

"It wasn't the right time until today. There is the Encaena celebration taking place in Feretrum. There are great crowds of visiting Anurans here in the coenobium. This is the long awaited day of retribution for what Feretrum did to us so many years ago. The time of cataclysm has arrived. There can be no more postponement or delay.

"So, you must allow me to take all of the ceratophrys at once. There is no time to lose. I must have it at this moment."

"But I still have frogs alive in the Sump," retorted Aptl. "They are not all dead yet. That has not happened as needed, but remains for me to complete. A lot of work still remains for me to complete."

"We can always return later and finish the rest off," lied Ranid. "There will be plenty of time for that later. Today, we will advance the main plan."

"Has Keigo Tragus been killed yet? I told Iwis not to take so much time for that task, but to have the hygeist called Omphal give him a lethal amount in a single dose. Who cares how it will look to outsiders once we have full control and make Iwis the new Mandator? The healer does not have to be so slow and meticulous in his killing of Tragus."

Ranid decided to venture another gambit. "We may need additional ceratophrys soon," he mumbled as if thinking aloud. "I have no doubt that we will need extra supplies of it before too long. The supplies will certainly fall very low as we use them up."

"I can get you more of it in the future," promised Aptl. "There are still many natural ceratoids underground in the subterrane beneath the soil. They grow and thrive like they do above ground. No need to worry, I tell

                         CLEMENT S. MASLOFF

you. There can be a lot more supplied in coming days. I know where they are and how to get my hands on them with ease."

"Ceratoids are small horned frogs and face many enemies," remembered Ranid from his wide reading in the librarium.

"The subterrane gives them protection," argued Aptl. "And I provide them plenty of food in the Sump. Iwis trusts me to take good care of these bane-makers that only we know are there. They are our hope for future victory and conquest. All our hopes of success lie with them."

Ranid and Ereth exchanged meaningful looks, each perceiving what the other was doing at the moment.

"What happens now?" asked the manager of the Frog Sump.

"We must go to the Encaena for the final battle," said Aptl. "On this day, the Gnomens will capture Feretrum. Our main weapon will be the killing ceratophys. Everything will then be in our hands."

Chapter XXIV

Early the next morning Ranid informed Glia what he had decided.

"It is a worthy goal for both of us," he said with a glowing grin. "Once we are married, that can become our main occupation and concern, helping to make the two streams into one big river. What can be a more elevated life goal for both of us?"

It took the couple a year after their wedding to formulate a shared theory of spiritual union. Copies of their principles of merger were distributed far and wide in the form of a small booklet. In a short time, both popular and scholarly interest in their ideas grew within both sects, the Anuran and the Salamandrine. Their message of unity and harmony had wide echoes in many regions and locations. It appeared to be what many thoughtful individuals in both of the streams were hunting for.

"We must make a wide tour of Salientia to spread our concepts of unification among Amphibiots of all persuasions," proposed Glia. "I believe that all the other Anuran coenobia would welcome us with friendliness. We can visit the best-known fanae and temples of this province and talk with many people who have written missives to us. There is much that we can learn through direct contact and conversation with potential followers."

Ranid suddenly recalled his own original background. "We will need Salamandrite support as well," he argued. "A wider swing will net us converts from both the camps. We need not be exclusively centered on one sect or the other. We must have the widest reach possible."

"That is right, my darling," she conceded. "We cannot be selective, but must try to be as inclusive as possible. No one can be omitted from our appeal and call."

The pair soon embraced, yet Ranid felt an interior uneasiness. It grew heavier all that day and through the following night. He found himself unable to fall asleep because of an undefined sense of guilt within him.

Ranid determined that he had to reveal the depth of his past affiliation in the capital to Glia. His conscience allowed him no alternative. He had been a fervent Salamandrite with a once promising future at the Archivum, a center of research and thought for that denomination. Integrity demanded that he inform his spouse of the strength of his earlier allegiance. How would she take his spiritual confession? How would his revelation affect their personal ties to each other?

The appropriate time for him to speak seemed to appear when the pair went into the cubiculum of the Mandator to describe for him their program of encouraging conciliation and tolerance between the adherents of the frogs and those of the salamanders.

Keigo Tragus listened with rapt attention to the prospective his daughter presented. He was sitting in a thickly cushioned wing chair in which he leaned further and further forward. There was a knotty problem for him in what Glia was saying. He decided to reveal it to the two younger ones.

"Like many attractive ideas, the ones that the two of you have reached is not capable of ever being realized. The people who follow the two differing systems are too settled in their ways and traditions. It would be an impossible surrender for either side to lose its identity in some general mix which would be neither the one or the other. No, neither group is willing to give up its most precious values. Everyone has to admit that such an amalgamation is inconceivable for both the one and the other. Especially for the leadership of the two streams, who would suffer great fear of losing their positions and advantages from any sort of merging or consolidation."

Glia's face reflected great distress inside her. "You do not wish to join with us in our campaign, Father?"

His eyes gazed at her with delicate tenderness.

"In my present position as Mandator, any thought of such radical thinking is impossible. I cannot stray into a new, different road," he sadly concluded. "It is too late for me. I made my choice long ago, and must live with it to the end."

The three of them were silent for a half minute or so. The father stared at his daughter, then Ranid. Finally, he addressed both of them at one time.

"Do what you think is right. No one has the authority to dissuade you from what appears to be your duty. That is what honor makes necessary for anyone with new ideas. You must both preach and propagate what you think and believe. I cannot make myself a part of your plan, though."

The young married pair soon left Tragus to his forlorn thoughts and regrets.

He could not make himself a part of their spiritual enterprise. They were now determined to leave Feretrum as soon as they could and take to the road as missionaries of a combinative, juncturist philosophy that had captured their minds and souls.

Ranid and Glia slowly crossed the Blackwater Swamp on a pair of old mules. They both became conscious of the unusual natural setting about them.

From a distant grove of smoketrees came the distinctive calls of an olive-green hortolani and a gray sora rail. A multicolored psittacine, hidden in the leaves of a striped zebratree, refused to join this general chorus of swamp avians.

Tiny tailless pikas and lagomorphs sped about among their hideouts with harelike velocity.

Apian bourdons buzzed around, transferring pollen from plant to plant. Frelonic hornets and guapes added their sounds to the symphony of nature.

The tiny moineau and gorrion birds appeared to be residents almost everywhere, as were also the corneille and the grive thrush. Whitethroat, redstart, and brantail warblers produced melodic snatches of song for the ears of Glia and Ranid. Goatsuckers and nightjars brought forth the sound of the whippoorwill. Pivets at work pecking away at trees were easy to locate by their noise.

The scarlet tanager and the golden oriole gave noticeable color to the scene the travelers passed. A few ruby-crowned kinglets drew surprised attention. The two trekkers identified meadowlarks and skylarks by their distinctive voices.

One day, the pair saw a large cigogne stork as well as a trochil hummingbird. That evening, the rossignol singing of a nightingale came to their ears. The mavis and the throstle were also audible. A rose-breasted grosbeak was sighted, as well as a dark purple starling. The tailorbird was seen in its nest of stitched leaves.

White plumes of wading flintheads and jabiru came into view. A jacana was seen walking over pond leaves on its long toes.

Large birds like the tall marabou and the quetzal drew their interest, along with the heavy toucan. The kagu flashed its bright red beak at the astonished human beings.

A fleeting idea occurred in the mind of Ranid. How would it be if the two streams of spirituality in Caecilia were based upon birds rather than amphibians like the frog and the salamander?

He smiled to himself as the notion evaporated out of his mind.

That was never to be, he said to himself.

Ranid and Glia arrived in Paludia after crossing the Blackwater Swamp in the solid darkness of night.

They were fortunate to find a tavern still open and rented a room there. Both were too tired to eat before taking to a wide, soft pilla bed and immediately falling asleep. Glia was first to awaken in the late morning. Ranid slept on in deep slumber, his body in an unmoving posture on the thick mattress.

Through the room window he could see a bellbird, rice bird, and budgerigah. All of them were loud and hungry.

Glia waited for him to become fully awake, amazed at how long he continued in a drowsy state. What is ailing him? she asked herself in wonder. Why is he so tired as this? Sitting in a chair of thatch, her gaze was glued to his sallow-looking face.

At long last, Ranid looked about without moving his head.

She bolted to her feet and rushed to his side. "How do you feel, my dear?" she asked. "Does anything hurt? You have slept the entire morning. I am a little worried about you."

"I feel chilly," he murmured weakly. "Why is it cold in this room?"

She did not answer at once, suddenly noticing that his upper lip was shivering. Her eyes looked at the parts of his body visible outside the bed cover.

Yes, there was visible trembling of his arms and feet. It was clear to her that he had fallen ill.

Glia felt a shudder down her back.

"I fear you have an ague, Ranid. Let me go and talk with the innkeeper. He can advise me if there is anyone who can be called to give you something. I'll return as soon as I can."

She went out of the bedroom with a shadow of fear over her heart. Was it a simple ague or something more serious and ominous? Glia asked herself.

Chapter XXV

Dr. Sural arrived at the inn the following morning. He was a short, tubby man with white hair and jade-colored eyes. His steps and movements were slow, nearly ponderous. As soon as he saw the sick traveler he made a diagnosis based on years of professional experience.

"Blackwater fever, that is what this is. You are an outsider, young man? This fever is endemic to our area. That is the kind of region we live in. Conditions have been like this as far back as historical memory exists. You are only in the first stage of the illness. There will be a period of temporary recovery, then a second stage will attack you with fury."

Ranid and the standing Glia gaped at the physician.

The face of the patient was deadly pale. His fingers were cold and white, the nails had a blue tinge to them. Ranid said nothing, remaining mute and wordless.

Sural turned to Glia. "Has he been urinating?"

"Yes," she replied. "I have taken his water with a small pot."

"It has come out clear, like clean water?"

"Yes, indeed," she answered, confirming his foreknowledge.

The doctor turned back to the sick man in the bed.

"In the second stage, your skin will burn and become flushed. This is the period of what is called dry heat. There will be little urination, and what there is will take on coloration that can alarm you. Do not be afraid, that stage will also pass by, though it will cause great pain for you. Patience is what is called for. You must allow nature to take you through a very torturous process."

Glia asked the physician a question next. "Can you give him something to alleviate the coming crisis he will have to go through?"

Dr. Sural slowly turned and faced her directly.

"I am sorry to have to tell you that there is no way to prevent the dry heat. A few alleviating pads can be placed on the skin at various points, but there is no medicine that can be applied at any stage of the illness. He must go through all three, however painful these turn out to be."

"What is the third period like?" demanded Glia, desperation in her voice.

"It is one of profuse sweating. Only after that can any recovery begin."

"And nothing can be done for him?"

Sural shook his head. "I shall bring some pads to use when I return later."

The medico excused himself and left.

Ranid soon fell into the second stage of Blackwater Fever, that of dry heat.

The physician returned with prepared pads to be placed at different points on the body of the tormented patient. Glia aided the doctor in this task. When they were finished, Sural spoke to her in a low tone as Ranid lay sleeping.

"This disease has been rampant for generations, but nothing to combat it has ever been found. It is a futile fight that gives me endless frustration. I wish that there was some weapon that I could use against this plague, but I know of none. No one has ever found a way to prevent the full course of the illness."

"It is a swamp fever?"

     CLEMENT S. MASLOFF

"That is the popular idea of this disease. But nothing is known about the cause."

She asked the question weighing most heavily on her mind. "Is this often fatal?"

His first response was a nod of the head. "In approximately half the cases. The outcome often depends on the strength of the body of the patient. That can be the primary variable."

Dr. Sural went away, promising that he would soon return to see the man in bed.

Glia sat down in a chair beside where Ranid lay. He began to mumble to her as if in delirium, as if asleep in a dream.

"There has to be some connective. Nature always creates something that serves as counteractant. Why is there no medicament, though? Something must exist, but where is it? If I recover my health, I will look for a curative. The people of this region need an answer to this. I will give them one, yes I will..."

The patient continued babbling in this vein. His body grew ever warmer.

At last, the dry heat stage began to disappear on its own.

Ranid and Glia both felt relief as his condition saw improvement.

When Dr. Sural returned, the one in bed was able to speak to him in a rational manner. "I have been considering what is to be done once this is past for me. My intention is to hunt for a remedy with which to fight this painful illness. That must be done, for I am certain that a solution is possible."

The physician bent forward, taking hold of Ranid's wrist in order to feel his pulse.

"For ages, we have tried to discover what can bring about a cure. But no one can determine whether there exists a single cause for this dreadful disease. The factor behind it remains a riddle."

"I promise that I will join that effort once I somehow escape the last stage."

The final, most dangerous phase of the illness descended upon the patient. Sweat poured over all portions of his body. His skin became drenched in the moisture exuded by him.

Glia used a pile of clean cloths to try to absorb some of the wetness. She bathed his limbs with clear water, yet the sweat continued to pour out of him without a stop.

He sporadically urinated into a pot that she held for him. A thick, brick-red sediment formed in the vessel, alarming her. She showed it to the doctor when he came back to examine the suffering Ranid.

"Hematuria," he told her. "Blood-filled urine is characteristic of this last, critical stage of the Blackwater Fever. That may be the derivation and the origin of the name of the disease. The great swamp that surrounds us on all sides may be the creator of all that is suffered by the victims."

Glia gazed down at the weakened Ranid, sharing in his pain and anguish.

All that anyone could do now was to wait for the finale of the physical crisis her husband was passing through.

The sweating came to an end and quick recovery of strength resulted.

Within two days, Ranid was on his feet again.

He had not forgotten the vow he had made to himself while under the fever.

"I must go out into the swales of the swampland and find out what can be learned about the terrible sickness that I went through," he revealed to Glia. "The object of my search will be unknown, of course, until I am fortunate enough to find what I am after. But I will surely recognize it when I meet with what I am after. Does that make any logical sense to you?"

What could Glia say in reply? She merely smiled with sincerity and warmth, yet not too hopeful that he would ever succeed in such a quest to find an answer to Blackwater Fever.

"Does our mission here to spread the message of conjoining the two streams of Amphibiotism into a single current continue? Are we going to attempt the recruitment of supporters in this area?" she inquired with visible anxiety.

"Of course," answered her spouse. "In fact, a discovery of the truth about the fever would bring a lot of attention and trust to our cause, that of spiritual unification of the frog and the salamander worshipers."

Glia nodded her forehead in agreement. "I see what you mean," she sweetly said to him.

The first local convert to Conjoinism turned out to be Dr. Sural himself.

It did not take a great deal of argument to convince him of the value of unity. He accepted the basic concept as if it were originally his own.

"Yes," he agreed. "That is the surest pathway to an end to this chronic conflict between the two strains of thought and belief. I have for years refused to identify myself with either. But a concordance around a general amphibianism will overcome doubts for both me and for many others at the same philosophical crossroads. Unity is the only possible solution."

Both Ranid and Glia rejoiced at this initial victory.

Sural invited them to stay at his cabin on the periphery of the town of Paludia. The two were able to look out the window into the Blackwater Swamp and take walks into it. One afternoon, while they were returning from a hike, Glia slapped the side of her neck.

"What was that?" inquired her mate.

"A gallinipper was biting at me and I wanted him to go away before he could do me great harm."

Ranid stopped, thinking a moment.

"The swamp is packed with them," he reflected. "They know what they want and like to hover close to where people are. We seem to offer an attraction to them."

"The pests want our blood," said Glia with a sneer for the mosquitoes.

"It is the female who does the biting," remarked Ranid. "I believe there are several varied species of them in the swampland. I wonder..."

He stopped, deep in inner thought.

"What is it that you wonder about?" she asked him.

"I have to ask Dr. Sural whether that insect could possibly act as contagium agent to transmit the fever through its bite. Does the gallinipper infect human targets with the disease when it takes blood?"

"That is an interesting question, Ranid."

"Let's go back and see whether we can find an answer to it."

 CLEMENT S. MASLOFF

Chapter XXVI

When the doctor returned from his medical rounds, Ranid made a direct inquiry of him on the veranda of Sural's cabin. The reply came at once from their host.

"I can truthfully inform you that neither I nor anyone else can answer that question. Maybe the mosquitoes are carrying agents of swamp fever, but maybe not. No one has ever studied them for that possibility. How could anyone study the flying dipterans in a scientific manner? I certainly don't know."

Ranid smiled with confidence. "I think that I'll let them practice biting on me," he confessed.

"You must not try anything risky or dangerous," frowned the host. "No one can be sure what the results might be."

Glia opened her mouth as if to speak, but was unable to say anything.

"Do not worry, I will take care of myself," promised Ranid. "If I locate and identify the causal factor, then a cure for the fever will be all the closer to realization. I am an optimist about success in achieving that."

A discovery can occur as a sudden, instant stroke when least expected.

An ordinary statement by Glia during the bathing of Ranid in a large tub set him on the trail of a thoughtful explanation.

"I see three insect bites on your back, up near your shoulder," she observed. "Do they hurt? Do they itch?"

"Don't touch them," he instructed her instantly.

"I would imagine that you were attacked by hungry gallinippers," she told him off-handedly. "Perhaps some rubbing cream or ointment might help you live with those awful bites."

The suddenly surprised mind of Ranid mulled over the condition just described to him by Glia.

When he was finished bathing and drying himself, he spoke to Glia on the subject she herself had brought up.

"Do you think that an insect like a mosquito could act as contagium of the Blackwater Fever?" he asked her, gazing deeply into her eyes.

She realized how serious this question was for him.

"I can't say, Ranid, because I don't know. My knowledge of nature is a limited one. But I know one person who can give us answers on these matters."

"Who is that?" he eagerly asked his wife.

"Ereth," she answered. "If we go back to Feretrum, he could tell us all that he knows about gallinippers. I am certain he would want to assist us on such a matter."

He considered what to do, biting his lower lip.

"I can make the best time there and back if I travel by myself. It can be completed in a few days, at top speed."

"What will I be doing all alone here?" asked Glia.

He gave her an understanding, sympathetic smile.

"Hold down the fort here, my dear. Keep your eyes open and note down the various characteristics of any new cases of fever that arise. I will go there and return in as short a time as I can make it. My plan is to take samples of the local gallinippers along with me for Ereth to examine and study. He should be able to determine whether my hypothesis about them is true or not."

 CLEMENT S. MASLOFF

She placed her right hand on his.

"My heart and mind will be traveling with you, my dear Ranid. When do you intend to leave for Feretrum?"

"As soon as I have collected enough samples of the flying insects. My hope is that this is not a ridiculous idea I have hatched. If it is, we shall soon find that out."

Glia, resting in his close embrace, kissed his lips.

"Take care of yourself," she said. "There is no need to try anything risky."

He nodded his head once, then picked up the large metallic box containing both dead and live mosquitoes.

In less than half a minute, Ranid was out of sight, making his way down the swamp path on the back of a trail pony he had rented from a swampman.

How is this venture going to end up? he asked himself again and again.

Ranid rode into Feretrum unnoticed. It was an evening of clear, star-filled dark sky. He dismounted and walked directly to the Frog Sump, finding Ereth at home in his small cabin.

The biologist was overjoyed to see that his friend had returned.

"This is a big surprise!" he said with a laugh. "How are you, and how is Glia? Where is she?"

The two men sat down. Ranid explained that he had journeyed here by himself. He then narrated the story of his severe Blackwater Fever and his difficult recovery. Then the traveler launched into his dream of defeating the scourge by searching for the cause in an unexpected direction.

"The concept of contagion resulting from gallinipper bites has captured my mind and imagination. Could the mosquito be the carrier of this dangerous disease? I ask myself a thousand times each day."

"I have never studied that insect as the cause of any infection," confessed Ereth. "But it strikes me as an idea worthy of attention and study." He suddenly, unexpectedly jumped up on his feet. "Let me get some books and manuals that describe these stingers in detail."

Most of that night, the two of them studied both the volumes and the mosquito samples brought there by Ranid. Short exchanges between them occurred at points of new, surprising interest.

"The entire family to which the gallinippers belong is covered by the name of culicines. Examining these many examples from the Blackwater Swamp, where you fell ill, I have to put these biters down as anophelines. These have the reputation of being aggressive and pesky pests, biting animals as well as human beings. Yes, these insects are known as fierce enemies of our own species. They can cause misery with their bites."

"But do they infect us with the awful Blackwater Fever?"

Ereth stared at him with a frozen look. "It is an explanation that makes sense, but cannot yet be confirmed. We have to look deeper into the question, and that may take us considerable time."

"But do we have the time for long, laborious research while the illness is still raging?" inquired an impatient Ranid.

The scientist looked down at the floor as if humiliated. "At times it may be necessary to act before enough knowledge has been found and collected. But I believe that there is already a way of wiping out the anopheline dominance in a swampy region. Their numbers could be greatly reduced today, even before we have scientific proof of their health dangers."

"How is something like that done?" anxiously asked Ranid.

Ereth opened a large, heavy book and found a page with illustrations. He pointed to a drawing of an odd-looking insect.

"This particular mosquito is a chaoborine, a very interesting one found in only a few areas of Caeclia. It has a special group of unique characteristics and could well hold the key."

"The key?"

Ereth turned his eyes back to the illustration in the book before him.

"Notice how the insect's body has only a few scales, unlike the anophelines. The mouth is small and not at all the piercing type most often found in other culicines.

"It is the larvae of the chaoborines that can be of critical importance to us. These strangely colorless creatures are predators. They destroy the larvae and adults of other mosquitoes and other small aquatic insects. Do you see what that means? Can you understand how significant it is?

"If the chaoborines were introduced into an area like the Blackwater Swamp, where they are at the present time unknown, they would soon cause a drastic change in the make-up of the overall mosquito population. A new balance between the species of insects would shortly arise. The number of anophelines would certainly fall precipitously, since they could not fight back against the strong, overpowering invaders, the warlike chaoborines.

"We would be able to measure a precipitous fall in the cases of Blackwater Fever, if your theory about the gallinippers is the correct one, my friend."

Ranid felt his heart pounding and his lungs working rapidly. His mind was excited with the new prospect just unfolded before him.

"But is what you say practical? Can it be done?" he asked the manager of the Frog Sump.

The biologist clenched his teeth. "With a lot of help, it can be achieved," he predicted.

Ereth went on to describe a plan of action against the anopheline gallinippers.

Chapter XXVII

"The best place to gather live chaoborines is here, on the Miasmic River," explained the biologist, pointing to an area on the wall map. This was where local villagers grew koksaghyz plants from which rubbery latex was obtained for all of Caecilia.

Ranid frowned upon hearing this. "It is so far away from the Blackwater Swamp," he protested. "How long will it take to complete our work here at Feretrum and journey there?"

"We will have to set off at once, as soon as all our preparations have been made. I have some large containers that can hold many live specimens. And a couple of sumpter mules will be needed by us."

"I can afford to buy several pack animals," announced Ranid. "Let's get what we need together. We should start out at once for this northern valley. You are certain it is the right place to capture these particular gallinippers?"

"Nowhere else are they as prevalent or available. It is worth the trip there and then back."

In three days, the pair left Feretrum for the Miasmic Valley, crossing scrub, brake, and quag on the way to the northern region of Caecilia. They skitted around the impossible region of chufa-growing Cienaga and the swampy marshes of Marecage. The quickest route for them was a circuitous, zig-zagging one. A straight line would have been futile.

Along the way, they met local Kroetes in villages such as Pantano and Marais, informing them of the basics of the Conjoiner views and principles.

   CLEMENT S. MASLOFF

Ereth, the biologist, surprised Ranid with his fervid adhesion to the new teachings of unity. "We must concentrate upon agreement and oneness," he told his traveling companion. "Since the universe we inhabit is not multiplex, neither can be our approach to the transcendental. Our perspective must remain a unifying one."

"That is the essence of our new philosophy," agreed Ranid. "I only hope that this journey will help to bring new recruits into our ranks. My dream is that the Conjoiners grow into a major force in the realm of the spirit, the we succeed in connecting what in the present is separated and divided."

The short man who came out of the tumble-down hut wore torn, shaggy shirt and pants. He eyed the two strangers carrying nets, moving closer to them.

"What are you up to?" the solitary asked them.

The answer came from Ereth, who was examining a bed of blue speedwell flowers. "We are gathering up local gallinippers for scientific research that has great importance. No harm will come to anyone from what we are doing, I assure you."

For a short time, the country recluse stared at the two travelers one-by-one, finally saying something to them.

"Forgive me if I seemed to be rude, but no one ever comes through here. My name is Dixo. For many years, I have been spending most of my time in meditation."

"You are a seeker of spiritual enlightenment, then?" said Ereth, his interest all of a sudden aroused.

"I did not start out as anything resembling that. I had my own retail business in Miasmic City. It was a false, hypocritical life that I was leading. There was no genuine happiness or satisfaction in anything that I did.

"One day, though, the thought of escape came to me. I decided that it had to be complete, total flight to be worthwhile. Nothing else could save me.

"So, I walked away from everything that encumbered me. Ever since then, my quest for meditative truth takes up most of my time, both day and night." He paused a moment. "Please excuse me, but I have to return to my train of thoughts and meditations. Not a moment can be wasted when such important and crucial concepts are being considered."

Before he could get away, Ranid managed to ask him one question.

"Could I visit and talk with you? I promise not to take too much of your valuable time."

A nod of the head was all the answer that Dixo gave or Ranid received.

As the mosquito-hunters walked away, Ereth muttered "What an odd character!"

Ranid arrived to see the hermit late the following afternoon, as twilight was beginning. The two men sat down on a fallen log beside a brooklet flowing between tall tacktrees.

"Tell me this: why do you and your companion go about collecting galinippers?" began Dixo.

It took several minutes for Ranid to cover the main aspects of the Blackwater Fever and the hope of doing away with the disease by replacing one species of insects with another.

But Dixo was most fascinated by a description of the Conjoiner principles by the missionaries and their message to both streams of Amphibiots.

"Explain the details of you teachings for me, please. I live by myself and see no one, so it is impossible for me to learn of such new and fascinating ideas as those which you espouse."

As Ranid furnished a general rundown of the unitary faith, The dark eyes of the lonely contemplator burned as if they were live coals.

"I see the sense and logic of what you teach, my friend. There can be no doubt that reason is with you and your colleagues."

     CLEMENT S. MASLOFF

The two stared at each other in silence, till Ranid had to change the subject.

"Can you tell me about how you go about meditating, Dixo?"

The latter briefly hesitated, then proceeded to reveal everything about himself.

"What does anyone start with? It has to be the self. That is what we entered this world with. So, a person focuses and concentrates, until the mind can go no further in that direction.

"When that pivotal point is reached, there occurs an inner explosion. One feels the joy of unlimited expansion of the soul. On and on this goes, until the soul engulfs the universal spirit, called by many the odyle.

"I have only reached that stage once, but it still remains my life's hope. That is the goal of all my meditation."

"You are very conscientious, Dixo," remarked Ranid. "I would like to learn much more about your methods. Show me how to do it, my friend."

The hermit nodded. "You will have to carry out the meditation by yourself."

Why must all living things come to an end in time?

Old age, illness, and death sweep away all humans. All living beings of this world disappear. Nothing is permanent.

Does anything at all transcend the reality that we see about us? Is there anything that has permanence? Some look to the frog, others to the salamander. These are mere traps for the mind seeking its liberation and illumination. One must forget the limits and boundaries set by the cults.

Attachments to such dogmas imprison both mind and soul of a thinker.

They divide a soul and separate person from person. These sects tie an individual to his own self.

In order to rise to higher, purer ideas we must be unattached to separate creeds. The odyle cannot be imprisoned in only one system.

Ranid realized that Dixo was a natural, self-made Conjoiner.

He and Ereth were in an inn on the periphery of Miasmic City.

"Soon we will have to leave," said Ereth one day. "We now have all the specimens of chaoborines and anophilines that can be used in trials in the Blackwater Swamp. We have really ended all our work hereabouts."

Ranid, all of a sudden, decided that this was the moment to outline a plan he had been formulating in his mind during his many conversations with the ragged meditator named Dixo.

"If our friend Dixo could be persuaded to travel with us back to the Blackwater region, he would certainly be a magnificent attraction and presenter of ideas. The man agrees thoroughly with our Conjunctionism."

"But I believe that he wishes to remain here as a contemplative recluse. Association with others does not attract his unusual soul. The man would surely refuse any such proposal."

Ranid smiled like a cat. "I believe that he can be convinced. Let me try."

That evening Dixo was informed that the day for departure was upon them. At first he looked perplexed, then worried.

"I hope that you continue with deep meditation on your own, Ranid," said the loner.

"If we took you with us, then you could continue to instruct me in the art of meditation. You would also have a lot of time for your own private thinking. We two could consult with each other as often as we wished.

"You know that I am a Conjoiner missionary. Our new movement needs its own meditative advisor. That can be you. We can bring difficult thought problems to you for advice. What do you say, Dixo?"

The latter was speechless only a short while. He soon accepted the offer that was presented to him.

 CLEMENT S. MASLOFF

Chapter XXVIII

After leaving Ereth at Feretrum, Ranid and Dixo continued on in the Blackwater Swamp.

Flocks of aquatic phalaropes flew up from their watery homes among the trees. The blackpoll, yellowhammer, anhinga, and ani flitted about in different directions, producing metal-like reflections. The sight was one of beautiful water fantasy, mesmerizing and enchanting.

The precious supply of mosquitoes slept in large boxes carried on mules supplied by Ereth. Slowly, the two travelers approached closer to their destination. They both grew impatient to get there.

But their arrival in Paludia was followed by an unexpected calamity.

Bad news was provided them by Dr. Sural, who greeted Ranid and his companion, the hermit, at the entrance to the inn where Glia was staying.

"She is ill with the fever," said the medico in a trembling voice. "Her illness is at the critical breaking point. It has reached its climax."

Ranid scurried to their room where his wife lay unmoving under layers of algodon sheets. Cooling perspiration gave a noticeable shine to her forehead.

Is she asleep? wondered Ranid, standing at her side.

All at once, as if sensing his presence, the stricken woman opened her eyes. With difficulty she recognized who had just entered the room.

Ranid bent over and kissed her on each of her swollen cheeks.

"I am back now," he whispered. "We will have enough new mosquitoes to destroy the ones that carry the fever. But you must get well. You will, I know that you will. Everything will be improving from this moment forward."

Glia opened her lips and began to purl forth into a gurgle. Finally, four words could be made out by her husband. "I love you, Ranid."

As if by themselves, the lids lowered over her swollen eyes.

He watched her closely for a long time. Dr. Sural brought a chair for him, and after a while he sat down on it.

All of a sudden, Ranid remembered the hermit he had brought back with him. In a whisper, he told the doctor that the man should be taken to a vacant room and allowed to rest up there.

"I have already done so," said Sural, making a sour face. "He told me that he is a Contemplator, whatever that is."

"I'll explain it to you later," replied Ranid.

"You must be hungry. I'll get you something to eat, and for the stranger as well."

The doctor left him staring at the afflicted Glia, suffering in pain.

The recovery of the patient was slow and difficult, but her body began to cure itself of the horrible Blackwater Fever. On the other hand, the successful introduction of chaoborines occurred swiftly and immediately. The expected results upon public health were clearly noticeable. Fewer and fewer cases of the fever were evident. The culprits of contagion, the traditional gallinippers of the region, were rapidly replaced by the newly introduced species.

The general public of all Caecilia learned of this triumph of biology through the popular press. Credit was given to the group that included Ereth, Sural, and Ranid. The latter saw to it that the victors were all identified as spiritual Conjoiners. The control gained over the fever was attributed to the inspiration received from the new, innovative philosophy of general unity and comity.

Within a short time, Ranid and Glia were once again traveling about on the road, spreading the happy message of Conjoinism among growing numbers of Amphibiots of both persuasions.

One morning Eleth appeared in Paludia when Ranid was there. At the entrance to the Conjoiner missionary office the two men embraced each other. Then Ranid took the visitor to the niche where he had his own whitewood desk.

Once the two were seated the biologist explained why he was there.

"I will soon retire from my Feretrum post at the Frog Sump. What I wish to do is make a contribution to our unification movement. And I think that I've conceived of a way of achieving some success for our cause."

"What is it?" asked Ranid with rising curiosity and interest.

Eleth made his mouth into a broad smile

"We call together everyone. Not only Conjoiners, but also the Salamandrites and the Anurans of all stripes. It is called the Great Assembly and is to be held in Caecilia City. This Unity Congress will be open to all ranks in all camps. No one will be excluded from either sect. Its objective is to be peace and brotherhood. If we are successful, the result will be the victory of our philosophy of spiritual oneness. We all are hunting for the odyle."

Ranid suddenly and unexpectedly leaped to his feet, surprising the other.

"The idea is brilliant," he boomed. "Let's go over to the publicity office and outline your plan to Dixo and his colleagues."

Eleth followed the exultant missionary out of his office.

Ranid told his two comrades the conclusions he had drawn from practical experience about the psychological effects of the Great Schism and the disunity and conflicts among Amphibiots.

"Where the Anurans are the dominant majority, they tend to become oppressive and masterful, even insolent, in action and manner. They swell up with self-regard and presumption. And I can attest that there is similar egotistic pride in the places where the Salamandrites prevail.

"On the other hand, when one of the spiritual movements is a small, weak minority, its members become abjectly secretive and self-deprecating. Experience has dispelled from my mind any doubts about these pernicious phenomena. They occur too frequently to be merely a random result of chance.

"I therefore conclude that the ancient division is a destructive influence on both majority and minority, both the dominant and subservient. Whatever the proportion in any particular place or region, all spiritual life will suffer from these tensions and problems.

"Neither side benefits from the endless schism."

Eleth then spoke up with a single sentence. "It is time for climactic action."

"You are right," agreed Dixo. "We must hold a unification congress for all of Caecilia. As I have said for many decades, the separation deforms both our doctrines. The result is distortion of spiritual truth on both sides. Fundamental asymmetry of thought occurs through the friction of argument and disputation. Both sets of teachings become partisan and partial. They are only the broken fractions of an invisible whole. The thinking of our brains becomes disfigured through having been dogmatized. Each separate philosophy is a misshapen one because of the intellectual war being waged during all this time. Their adherents all become victims of the conflict, on both sides.

"So, a convention aimed at unification is the only means of reforming millions of minds and spirits."

Ranid and Eleth did not add anything to what Dixo had put into words.

Their silence signified complete acceptance of all that had just been said to them.

     CLEMENT S. MASLOFF

A large meeting hall was needed in the capital where the convention could meet in safety and security. Ranid decided he had to go there to oversee the arrangements. It was almost seven years since he had seen his native city. He decided that the person he had to see first was Hyle Xalus, the Praeposter of the Salamandrine Archivum. There was no one else whom he trusted more than this loyal friend. Yes, he was certain that Hyle would be glad to help him obtain what he needed at this point in time.

They had not seen each other since Ranid had left Caecilia City as a fugitive. There had been no messages, no contact whatsoever. It was doubtful to him that Xalus knew of his involvement in Conjoinism. Ranid had always attempted to downplay his own name in the movement. Anonymity had been one of his main goals in all public appearances. He did not wish to enjoy any celebrity.

Had he kept himself in the shadows sufficiently so that his old enemies in the capital were unaware of his activity in the movement? Was he safe from the possibility of arrest on old charges from the early years when he had first become a questioner and heretic? These were vital questions he was unable to answer by himself.

Hyle Xalus would tell him much when they met after all that had happened since he had departed from the capital.

Both Ereth and Dixo had the desire to accompany him on the journey. But Ranid insisted it was best he went by himself, without a retinue of any sort about him. The trip was meant to be a short one. He planned to slip in, then out quickly. Nothing decisive was intended by the originator of the Conjoinist current of thought. The journey was to be merely exploratory.

Chapter IXXX

The streets of the great city appeared as drab and colorless as when he had left. For Ranid, it seemed that the past was returning to life. Memories remained fresh and strong. He recalled how he had visited the Praeposter that first time to apply for the job in the Archivum. This time his purpose was quite different. How would his mentor receive him after years of absence? Have critical changes of some sort occurred?

He knocked at the door. When a young aide appeared, Ranid identified himself and asked to be announced to the head of the Archivum. The puzzled assistant disappeared. When the door again opened, it was an older Hyle Xalus who stood there peering at him.

"Ranid! I could not believe it was you. First of all, let me welcome you back. Come with me to my sanctum. The two of us must talk. It has been a long time since you and I have been together."

When they were seated and alone, Hyle began to question his surprise visitor.

"Why have you never written to me? Did you ever try to communicate? Many times I have thought of looking for you, but never did. Let me tell you this: your offenses against the Capitular, Caudo Eximius, are all but forgotten and erased. I have campaigned for your rehabilitation. You are now safe here in Caecilia City. There are no existing charges or accusations against you, I am confident. But it has not been possible to inform you of this development."

Ranid, sitting opposite his former employer, made a sour grimace. "Does Eximius still exercise total domination over all the Salamandrites through his Apodist secret cabal? Does that remain the pattern of power here? Has there been any change whatever?"

Hyle gave a sad nod of the head. "His will is absolute. He decides the form that all scholarship must take. Nothing sees the light of day without his approval. It has become even worse than it was when you were here, my dear fellow. We are living under a tyranny within the Salamandrine faith. All thought is under strict, tight control."

"He has a personal dominance over all the salamander-worshipers, then."

The Praeposter bit his lip. "I resist that yoke, as I have always done. But my opposition has to remain silent and invisible. There has been no opportunity to act together with others. We are unseen and unheard of in our disgust with his system of domination and authority."

Ranid decided to describe his recent history to the archivist.

"I am no longer a Salamandrite. My present position is in a new stream, that of the Conjoiners. Have you heard of our movement and its progress?"

Hyle looked surprised. "You are one of them?"

"I am in the top leadership. They have sent me to Caecilia City with a special mission. We need one of the largest auditoriums for a national convention aiming at the goal of spiritual unity. Could you help me obtain access to a giant hall like the Hypogeum? That will be of great importance to the future of all Amphibiots."

The older man grinned. "I am familiar with the pamphlets of your new group. Its ideas are extremely attractive. I am favorably impressed by everything that I know about your small sect. In a way, I am no longer the kind of Salamandrite that I once was in the past. Our organizational structure is a fossilized skeleton with little life in it. I have become a mere time-server in a musty relic which is no longer what it once was. We live today within a different environment, not the old one. Everything within our lives has become oppressive."

Ranid opened his mouth to voice his agreement with the feelings the other was expressing, but Hyle beat him to it with a surprising proposal.

"The Hypogyeum would be an excellent site. Why don't the two of us go and have a look around about the place? That will give you some ideas to take back to your associates, and I myself can talk to its managers about the terms under which they might rent it out. My aim will be to win the best conceivable terms for this convention that is being planned."

As the two walked along together through alleys behind buildings that fronted on major streets of the capital, Hyle described what he had been engaged in for the last several years.

"My interest in the Institutor, Alsike Caldus, has come to center on the years of the Great Schism and the way in which he negotiated his way through the storms and catastrophes of that contentious time.

"I have found archival correspondence that Alsike carried on with potential supporters and allies, as well as individuals distancing themselves from him. At first, it was a complex, confusing kaleidoscope of contending persons and ideas. But I am beginning to perceive certain repeated patterns and designs. The picture is starting to make sense to me.

"For instance, Alsike very often treated colleagues the opposite of what might logically be expected. If a corresponding acquaintance believed his own ideas were identical to those of the Founder, he would try to reveal and emphasize differences instead. And if someone wrote in opposition to him, Alsike usually highlighted the great degree of agreement between them, masking and disguising their contradictions.

"And this proved to be a good method of keeping himself as the focus of all thought about the odyle. But it also made my research very difficult, for I was compelled to probe into why he was saying a certain thing at a specific time, in a missive to a particular person with this or that background.

"The protean nature of all his serious correspondence can result in mind-twisting puzzles. My research often turns into an exercise in the solution of deep riddles. I have found it extremely hard to fit all the parts and pieces together into a harmonious system. It is nearly an impossible task to complete."

               CLEMENT S. MASLOFF

Once the scholar became silent, Ranid decided to give an opinion of his own.

"Yes, Alsike often seemed to weave and bob about during the period of the schism between Salamanderism and Anuranism. He could not have predicted at the time how many problems this would present for future followers or for the researchers trying to understand how things happened."

Hyle frowned. "The hardest nut to crack is the correspondence between Caldus and Vahid Devro, the first true Anuran. I still struggle to grasp what each of them meant in the letters they exchanged in those momentous years back then."

Ranid smiled and nodded his head. "I can sympathize with anyone who delves into their correspondence. One has to have both patience and sensitivity for such a difficult task as that."

~

The Hypogeum hall was reached by various stairwells that went down into the subterrane. The auditorium was enormous, at least a hundred and fifty cubitals from side to side. Its dome was very dramatic in design. Ranid surveyed the vast space with awe.

"What do you think?" asked Hyle. "Will it hold all who want to be here?"

"Certainly. It will encourage many to travel long distances to participate."

"If only these sessions turn out successful. So much depends on what is going to happen here," quietly meditated the Praeposter. "To give a coloring of safety to this unity convention, I will make the contract for the place in the name of the Archivum. That will give it a legitimate color."

"Thank you," said Ranid. "That is most generous of you."

"We can head back to the Archivum now. There are some documents concerning the Institutor, Alsike Caldus. I am certain they hold great interest for you, my friend. Nothing like them has been uncovered before."

"I will peruse them later," promised the missionary. "My immediate objective is to look about the Hypogeum in order to test the acoustical characteristics of the building. We can meet at the Archivum later."

The pair took leave of each other. Ranid went up on the main platform in order to test how sound carried from there to the farthest corner.

Two men took hold of Ranid from both sides as he climbed up the stairwell.

One of them wore canary yellow, the other a vitelline yellowish-red shell jacket.

"Come with us," muttered the senior uniformed officer.

"Am I under arrest?" reacted Ranid. "Are the two of you public police?"

Neither made any reply as they guided their prisoner to the rear of an unmarked van and deposited him on a bench inside.

"Where are you taking me?" demanded the arrestee.

Neither of his captors answered. Soon the vehicle was leaving its location above the Hypogeum hall. Several quick surmises materialized in the mind of the prisoner. These two men were Salamandrite guards, with as much public authority as any state police. Where were they taking him? To the castellum headquarters of the cult, to where the Capitular exercised absolute power? To where that single person was the superior of everyone within the overall organization?

There was no answer from anyone to the burning questions on his mind.

Where were the public circles that controlled the policing power?

To the castellum headquarters of the sect, to where the old Capitular exercised authority over the members. That was where they were taking him.

Ranid had to come to only one possible conclusion: somehow, agents of the Capitular had caught sight of him.

Perhaps these men had been watching the Archivum and saw him enter, then come out again with Hyle Xalus. However it happened, he was now a captive. What was the best reply when they asked him what he had been doing the past seven years? How was he to protect himself?

                    CLEMENT S. MASLOFF

Spiritual searching and meditation, that was the best alibi and excuse. Not a word about his missionary work as a Conjoiner. Nothing definite about his new specific orientation. No such identification or connection.

Could he succeed in pulling off such a justifiable deception? he wondered.

Chapter XXX

R anid trembled when he thought of questioning by the Capitular himself.

It would be a bitter contest of wits between the two of them. The van they were in stopped and the prisoner prepared to climb out of it.

The cuddy used in his interrogation was ridiculously small, yet bright with concealed sources of light. Ranid sat in an old pilaster chair. His several questioners always stood directly in front of him. None of them ever sat down to rest.

Several times exactly the same inquiries were made of him.

What was his true name? Where had he been the last seven years? How had he been earning his living? Who were his closest associates? Why had he come back to the city he had fled from some time ago?

Ranid gave his name and nothing beyond that. He demanded to know why he had been picked up and brought here. What were they after from him? he asked. What was the nature of the accusations and suspicions concerning him? When did they intend to release him? Could he send out any kind of message to anyone he wished to communicate with?

His intransigent attitude aroused the ire of each griller who entered the tiny chamber. But he knew what he was waiting for: the appearance of the Capitular to take his turn in dealing with this difficult prisoner.

It became evident to Ranid that the day had ended and that night had fallen. How had Hyle Xalus reacted to his failure to return? Had he understood the seriousness of what had happened to his long-lost friend?

     CLEMENT S. MASLOFF

A rest period was given to him. A container of menthe tea was provided to quench his terrible thirst. He could relax a little, although his sense of tension and danger was very high.

He made a guess as to who would be appearing there soon: the top man in the Salamandrine hierarchy.

As soon as he entered the interrogation chamber, the tall, commanding figure was recognizable. He no longer was the same thin and gaunt Capitular as years before. With passing time, his weight had radically increased. The man could only be described at present as grossly fat and unhealthy.

The sherry eyes of the executive had not lost their sharpness of focus.

A smile came to the lower face of the supreme official of the Salamandrites.

"It is good to see you once again, after so much time. What is it that you have been doing all these years, may I ask?"

"I have been like everyone else in this land of ours, hunting for spiritual revelations and solutions. Isn't that what all men and women are seeking?"

The Capitular stopped smiling in a fraction of a second.

"I offered you so much, yet you ran off in refusal. Your behavior was not at all easy for me to understand. Your career in our ranks would have been guaranteed and assured, but something made you go in an opposite direction. Your motives at that time were a total mystery to me. They still remain that."

Ranid lowered his voice as if fearful of being overheard.

"I could not become a pretender or counterfeiter like some do. How could I claim to be a traditionalist in the Salamandrine vein while also belonging to an arcane inside cult that was centered upon the Apod? No, I could not become that kind of faker. My conscience did not allow me room for such supreme hypocrisy."

Caudo Eximius glared at him with his anger barely controlled.

"Do you dare call Alsike Caldus, our Institutor and Originator, a dealer in fraud? Is that what you dare to say?"

"I believe it is you and the Apodists who make such an inference possible," shot back the prisoner. He suddenly decided to be more cautious in his statements to this authoritative figure at the top of the hierarchy.

But the face of the Capitular continued to blaze with stark fury.

"Do not think that I know nothing of your activities, first with the Anurans of Feretrum, then more recently as the main missionary of this new, combined sect, the Conjoiners. I have been receiving detailed reports on you. Your crimes are an open book to me. I am aware of the entire story of your madcap wanderings. Nothing can be hidden from me."

Ranid gasped in surprise. "You know what I am attempting to do here in the capital?"

The official nodded yes. "In fact, I do not plan to impede your convention in the Hypogeum. Why should I do that? It is all going to turn out favorable to the special, inner organization that I head. Our hidden power is not going to be damaged at all. The existing balance of forces will continue as it has."

"How is that assured you?" said Ranid excitedly. "I am not about to become your agent within the Conjoiner ranks, sir."

"This is your second chance, young man," archly whispered the Capitular. "There will be no third one for you. I assure you of that."

The two exchanged bold stares, each taking the measure of the other one.

"I would like to go back to the Archivum," said the prisoner. "It has been years since I worked there. It was a site of profound happiness for me."

"You are free to leave here and go wherever you please," said the now heavy man with an evil grin on his face.

⌒

     CLEMENT S. MASLOFF

The Praeposter and his former assistant talked long past midnight after the latter was released by the highest Salamandine authority.

Xalus surprised Ranid by describing a series of letters he had recently come upon in forgotten, obscure collections.

"We know that in the Age of Schism it was common for those who wrote to others on spiritual and philosophical topics to disguise their identity with a pseudonym or allonym from someone else's name. One has to take care to decipher who it is standing behind this or that false designation. Unconscious marks of style can often indicate the true identity of the real writer, and I have tried to use them to find out how Alsike Caldus signed the correspondence originating with him.

"I told you, Ranid, of a most interesting letter that was received by the Institutor, expressing profound agreement with his hypostatic interpretations. This intrigued me, so I devoted a lot of time to pinning down the actual author. From mannerisms and hints, I had to conclude that it was Vahid Devre, the man who at that time was setting the groundwork for the rise of Anunanism.

"You must read a copy of this communication that I transcribed from the Devre letter. The importance of the message will be evident to you at once."

Xalus rose to his feet and went over to a metallic box lying on a table. Out of it he took out a cartonboard folder full of papers. Moving back, he handed it to Ranid.

The latter opened what he had been given, finding a five-paged letter inside. He began to read with increasing slowness, analyzing each word and phrase. Finally, he looked up at Xalus, standing beside the chair he sat in.

"This is quite meaningful, I believe," admitted Ranid. "If this truly came from Devre, it means that the Founder previously wrote him an original exposition of his deepest views on how the divine odyle came to be incarnated in amphibians. Nothing like that has ever been seen or referred to, as far as I know."

"What has become of the prior communications that Alsike sent to Devre?" Xalus made an enigmatic grimace, neither a smile nor a frown. "No one can say for sure, of course, but they may still survive."

"But where?" eagerly asked Ranid.

"The greatest probability is in the Devre family archive. Anurans have never collected all the correspondence of their creator within the central records of their association. It is entirely possible that letters from Alsike Caldus were signed with a pseudonym that no one, down to this day, has recognized or decoded. Since we have in our Archivum the response from Devre himself, there has never been any way for the scholars on their side to perceive or understand the importance of something which only acquires significance when its writer is identified. It's this separation of the two missives that conceals what they really are about."

"The whole situation is an impasse, then," sighed the Conjoiner. "If only it was possible to look through the papers of the Devre family!" He pondered this difficulty, when a wild idea struck him. "Wait a moment," he said, rising to his feet, reaching into his inner coat pocket, and removing his money wallet. A folded card was located, then taken out.

"This is my entrant card when I joined the Anuran community at Feretrum. There is some chance that this can get me into the family archive, isn't there?"

Xalus looked astounded. "You went into their organization?"

Ranid nodded that he had.

"I have been both a Salamandrite and an Anuran," he explained. "But now I am a unifier, one of the Conjoiners. Nothing beyond that."

"And you still hold your old identifier?" asked Xalus with astonishment.

"I forgot that I was carrying it on me. Hopefully, that card can now be of practical use to me. It can perhaps open the Anuran archives to what I am after."

"You are willing to attempt this?" said Xalus with excitement on his face.

"Why not? A probe might end in success."

 CLEMENT S. MASLOFF

"When will you start, Ranid?"

"As soon as possible, tomorrow morning."

Chapter XXXI

The centuries-old house had high gables with antique lucarne windows. It showed signs of the warping and decaying inevitable with age. There was an historical aura about the almost decrepit place.

Ranid stopped on the street cobbles and looked up at the pigeons along the slate roof. This is where Vahid Devre once lived, he said to himself. This is where that great man's personal archive is located. What might be learned among the surviving papers and documents in the obsolete building?

With mild trepidation, he went to the heavy front door and rapped the marteau. A tall man in a servant's formal dark suit appeared.

"I am a historical researcher and wish to see the person in charge of the Devre family archive," explained the smiling young man just off the street. "It is important for me to receive access to certain old letters from the past. They could be of enormous value in the writing of history and biography of the time of Amphibiot formation and organization. That is why I have come here today."

The suspicious butler looked into the face of the stranger, then examined him from head to toe.

"Step into the alcove and wait," he indicated, retreating in order to make way. "I shall report your presence to the mistress and she will speak with you. All important decisions are in her personal hands."

Ranid entered the nogal-paneled vestibule of the old building. He only had to wait seconds before a tall, middle-aged woman in a dark blue algodon dress appeared. Black hair had strands of gray in it. Milky blue eyes shone

     CLEMENT S. MASLOFF

with lively intelligence. Although this woman was so different in looks from his own Glia, there was a spark in her eyes that reminded him of his spouse.

"Yes," she began, "can I be of help to you?"

He addressed her in a mild, petitioning voice.

"My name is Ranid Rolius. I am a member of the Anuran convent community at Feretrum, and my purpose here today is purely one of historical scholarship. Let me explain.

"The life of Vahid Devre has been studied by many historians and biographers, using the archive in this residence. For me, the period of special interest is that immediately prior to the Great Schism. There was much correspondence between those who played roles in that drama of the past. That was an era when frequent letter-writing was the custom. Much of it survives.

"My attention focuses upon a number of those who were in touch with that great pioneer of Anuranism. I am especially concerned with the letters that may have been sent to Vahid Devre by a philosophy student named Emon Lannus. I wish to find and study the missives that man may have sent to the founder of Anuranism."

The tall woman made an undecipherable grimace.

"I am the sole living descendant of Vahid. My name is Dera Devre, and I am the person in charge of all family records and documents. Let me tell you this: I do not recall any letters from an individual with that name. What was it again?"

"Emon Lannus," answered Ranid, repeating the pseudonym used by Caldus so long ago as the Great Schism was approaching.

"I cannot remember such a correspondent," remarked the woman. "If the person was someone of importance, it would surely have left a mark in my memory. Yet I have a blank gap on any such letters. Why do you believe this exchange occurred, may I ask?"

"There are existing letters from Vahid Devre to the person called Emon Lannus. That would indicate that others written by this unknown person may still survive here in what was left by the great founder. At any rate, I think it useful to make a search for that purpose. They may be or not be available to peruse and read. But that cannot be determined at this time, till the correspondence is examined and studied."

Dera Devre gave him a searching, probing look, as if looking for some significant clue.

"I am not certain," she suddenly told him. "Give me a day, and I shall give you an answer tomorrow," she said with a face of stone.

Ranid frowned sadly. "I do not have much time here in the capital, for it will be necessary before too long for me to leave on other duties."

For a time, she said nothing. Her mind rapidly considered alternative replies.

"Come in and be seated in the parlatorium while I have a look in the catalog file for that particular name. It may be that I have forgotten or overlooked it in the past. There is no way of knowing for certain till a search occurs."

Ranid stepped out of the alcove into the reception salon of the house. It was an old-fashioned, ornate room with satin wall murals and flowery furniture. He took a plush cushion-chair and waited, gazing at the richly wainscoted ceiling and wall bolserie.

Who can today afford such expense? wondered the visitor with a sigh.

His wait turned out to be a short one. Dera entered and gave him good news.

"I found that person's name among the listing for secondary correspondence," she announced. "There are a number of letters, some quite long. Do you have a particular month or day in mind from what you know about the other end of the exchange?"

Suppressing his sudden joy, Ranid gave her a precise date.

"Come with me," she ordered him. "There is an empty cubicle that you can use. I will locate the folders holding these letters and bring them up for you to see."

Ranid wrote verbatim copies of each page on paper furnished him by Dera Devre. He was able to identify instantly the passages written by Asdike Caldus that represented the core of the future schismatic split.

"...though it saddens me greatly, I must point out the unacceptable portions of your spiritual philosophy. Silence for the sake of good manners is without value in such a situation. Complete candor is the only way to advance the search for higher truth. I must be completely candid. That is my duty.

"First of all, both of us agree that whatever it may turn out to be, the Divine is closely connected to the universe that you and I inhabit. That is a self-evident truth. Our differences surface when we attempt to describe and define the central nexus of all existence and being.

"By this time we all recognize that it is an amphibian that serves as the mundane incarnation and symbol of the Ineffable. The indefinable, indescribable Odyle, or odic being, is presented to us through what may be termed its avatar. As you know, there is growing disagreement over what particular amphibians act in this capacity in place of the Supreme Being. There are those who adhere to the frog, but there also exists solid support for choosing the salamander. This is an ominous, most serious divide that must not be allowed, at any cost, to expand or consolidate. In recent days the idea of a solution has come to me.

"Each individual must undertake a lifetime journey to reach the odyle alone. Direct contact and unity is the supreme good, the final end and destination.

"If we come to see the various amphibians as possible bridges to a mystical linkage, to ultimate bridging over, then they will take their rightful place as means, and only means, to the Highest Level, the Transfinite.

"Let me say it this way: the frog and the salamander are only hypostatizations of what each of them represents and symbolizes. They share much with the Divine, but are not themselves such. They can be defined as incarnating avatars, but no more. With all their spiritual value, they cannot rise to the odic level in any way, because of their worldly, material natures. They serve because of the invisibility of the Sublime that is reflected in them.

"In a strange way, the amphibians are reflections of the Transfinite.

"Both salamanders and frogs act as such for us. Why should either be preferred?

"It would be best to combine all the amphibian avatars into a single framework of ideas and worship each and every one of them equally and impartially.

"That is the difficult task that deserves to be worked out in the future."

Ranid stopped writing and set down his stylo. His eyes rose and he studied the sapinwood ceiling.

The inescapable conclusion was plain and clear to him.

Alsike Caldus had been a pre-Conjoinist unifier, a Conjoiner before the third stream ever saw daylight.

He was an unknown, unidentified Conjoiner before any others existed.

But in the course of the Great Schism, a turn in another direction occurred. Why was that so? Ranid could conceive of no simple explanation. Perhaps in the debates and battles of that time, each side mobilized itself for combat, for spiritual warfare.

Caldus and Devre had become personal enemies. Opposed movements had coalesced around each of them. Militancy and fanaticism arose and strengthened. Polarization and tension resulted. Is there any surprise that Alsike was compelled by circumstances to forego the chance of advancing to a higher level of understanding? That he was forced to speak in the name of a partial viewpoint, not a universal perspective? That he gave up the highest possible understanding that he had attained, and lowered himself to the partiality of partisanship?

Conjunctive amalgamation was forgotten, set aside as a speculative venture whose time had not arrived.

     CLEMENT S. MASLOFF

Over and over the letters went Ranid, reading how two allies evolved into enemies.

Chapter XXXII

On his second visit to the residence, Dera invited him to have jasminoid tea with her in the small recessed galleria displaying works that she herself had painted.

"I never suspected that you were a visual artist," he exclaimed as he sat down at a round table. The hostess smiled at him for the first time.

"That has long been my hobby and main amusement."

She poured him hot liquid from a steaming warmer, filling his dainty little tasse with tea.

"What made you turn toward landscape of the swamplands?" he asked, taking his cup and noiselessly sipping.

"Perhaps it was my interest in the wide diversity of frogs and toads," she replied. "There was a magnetic attraction that drew me at the time. My ambition to paint developed as if on its own. The process was almost unconscious, I believe."

"Interesting, very interesting. But I do not see amphibians at all in any of your paintings. Why was it that they seem to have been omitted from your subjects? Why did you primarily draw trees and water in still perspective?"

All of a sudden, the smile vanished from her face.

"When I was younger, there was much more spiritual interest in me than in later years. For some reason, my old spirit seems to have waned. Of late, I rarely draw the amphibians. And me a descendant of Vahid Devre! Who would have thought that would happen?"

     CLEMENT S. MASLOFF

"I would not worry about that," he comforted her. "Many people have spells of distance and then closeness. These can come and go, just like a cycle."

"That is one way of putting it," she thoughtfully agreed. "Yes, you speak deep wisdom. Tell me this: have you experienced high and low points of spirituality?"

Ranid sensed a warning emotion pulsating inside him.

What should he say to her? How much could he afford to reveal to someone he did not know with any familiarity?

"Mine is not so much an up-and-down fluctuation, as a refining of focus. It is hard for me to explain, even to myself. But of late, I find that my interest becomes ever more general, more abstract and theoretical. I become more philosophical all the time. I do not know where the trend will carry me. All I can say is that an unknown current is bearing me forth."

Have I said too much? he wondered. Have I confused this heiress to the Anuran tradition?

The woman called Dera appeared to take all he had told her in stride.

"Yes," she returned,"that is precisely what I feel is happening to me, too."

Was she moving toward Conjoinism? he asked himself.

The two finished their tea, then Ranid left for his room at the depot hotel.

Once the date for the convention at the Hypogeum was firmly set, hordes of members and sympathizers began to congregate in Caecilia City.

They came by magneto-train, horse wagon and coach, river boat, and road cart. Small, circular green and yellow badges were distributed to identify the Conjoiners and their supporters. All hotels, hostels, lodges, and rooming houses ended up packed with patrons. The streets, avenues, and boulevards of the metropolis appeared to be extraordinarily crowded. Large throngs of enthusiasts came to have a look at the underground hall where deliberations were slated to be held.

None of the permanent residents of the city had ever seen anything like it.

Particular restaurants, tea rooms, taverns, and shopping arcades became favorite spots for the Conjoiners to gather in informal assemblies.

Who could stay unaware of what was happening in their midst?

The two established sects, the Salamandrites and the Anurans, made continued reports about the oceanic wave of heretics to their respective leaders.

Both organizations began to mobilize, for they knew not what was coming.

Caudo Eximius, the Capitulator, continued to be the calmest among all the Salamandrine upper hierarchy. The tall, emaciated leader gave commands in a composed, level voice to his subordinates gathered in his sanctum at the Citadelle. All twelve of them listened obediently to his words as if expecting final elucidation of the situation they faced.

"When one is facing fools like these dissenters, actions cannot be precipitous. There is never any advantage when you move too hastily or without thorough forethought. No, we have to be as watchful as possible and have our eyes open for the perfect opportunity that fits our needs."

A unanimous murmur of assent greeted this sentiment of the sectarian head.

"One must develop the ability to perceive and understand fatal errors in your foe when they occur," continued Eximius, his voice reverberating a little louder as he went on. "That is a very important point for each of us to consider, for we all know how stupid these heterodoxers are, else they would not be involved in such insane mouthings or the frolics they are about to commit in the Hypogeum. Our task is to watch for the inevitable flaw and pounce upon it at the appropriate moment."

He paused several seconds, as if for effect.

"There are several Salamandrine youths, recent initiates, who have volunteered to attend this lunatics' convention and report back to me what they hear and see there. These people, though only a few, have been trained to be watchful and attentive to everything going on about them. They will be sitting with the sympathetic general public and will inform us what happens in the hall."

All of a sudden, Eximius smirked with an indefinable emotion.

"There are other alternatives that I plan to explore, but cannot go into now," avowed the chief of the Salamandrine movement.

Dera only occasionally saw her one brother, Talem. His visits to the old mansion were infrequent, a fulfillment of filial duty to his one and only sibling. Why did he drop by to see his sister on the eve of the great Conjoiner meeting? Perhaps his unconscious goal was something as intangible as obtaining some inspiration from being inside the historic family homestead.

Tall and thin, with the same milky eyes as Dera, this younger brother always provided her an interval of pleasure that broke the monotony of her days.

The pair sat down at a small mensal in a kitchen alcove.

"You look well," said Talem warmly. "What are you doing to give you such a boost in your attitude and appearance?"

She gave a brief, clipped laugh.

"There is nothing particularly different in my schedule to make any visible change in me. But there is one new matter here in the house. I have had a scholar coming to search through the Devre archives. This person makes copies of letters in the files of Vahid Devre. He is very enthusiastic about what he is doing, I can tell each time that he visits."

"That is interesting," said her brother. "What is the fellow's name?"

"Ranid, he is Ranid Rolius. He is a member of the Anuran spiritual community at Feretrum and appears to be enlightened and inspired."

"Feretrum? I have heard that there have been troublemakers there. Even their Abbot has been implicated in a new heresy. Many say that Conjoinism started there at Feretrum."

The sister pursed her thin lips. "I have not heard anything about that from Ranid," she told him in a lowered tone.

"Perhaps these recent changes out there have no connection to this scholar," mused the brother. "Who can say?"

Dera attempted to change the subject.

"Is there a danger of physical conflict with the heretics assembling in Caecilia City?"

He beamed her a smile. "No one can predict how things will turn out, but we are quite confident. All five of the Anuran syndics are united in their determination not to give an inch of concession to the dissidents. Their aim is to wear them down, in time."

She smiled at him. "You are most well-informed, serving the Board of Syndics as Chief Secretary."

"Indeed, I am at the center of communications within our organization. That furnishes me an excellent vantage point for observing events as they occur."

"I am proud of you, Talem," she said tenderly. "They will some day choose you to become a syndic, I am certain of that. It is only a matter of time."

All at once, Talem made an unusual request of his sister.

"Dera, I am eager to learn what this provincial scholar may be studying and what he has found. Is there any record of the letters he has perused and made copies of?"

She thought for a moment.

"I made marks on the catalog cards that indicate which documents he took to read."

"That would be one way of going back to specific letters and finding out what drew his attention." Talem sprang to his feet. "I think I will go and have a look. You can stay here and wait for me. I will report to you if I uncover anything of interest in the family archive."

Talem climbed down to the family archive chamber. He was familiar with all of its treasures, having spent many hours there over the years.

He went at once to the catalog box and found there the list of letters received by his famous ancestor. As Dera had told him, some of them had small check marks recently made.

The Anuran bureaucrat went to the letter files and searched for specific numbered folders. Taking several of interest, he moved to a desk and began to look these over.

Instantly, his attention was riveted by the content of the messages from an unknown writer, one with an original, agile mind. But the handwriting was one he recognized. He had seen the same distinctive chirography and style in historical documents of the Age of Schism.

Talem realized at once that these letters could ignite an explosion.

Chapter XXXIII

Alarge salon in the Traveler's Hotel at the Magneto-train Depot was rented for a strategy conference of the most prominent leaders of the Conjoiner movement. This hotel was a cement structure situated above the station and the rail tracks.

Eretho, Dixo, Sugal, and Ranid sat at a long pigwood table facing the room full of activists.

Dixo called the session to order and proposed that Dr. Sugal preside as chairman. The latter rose to his feet and began the business of the meeting.

"I have the honor of asking Mr. Ranid Rolius to address us about a recent discovery he has made while engaged in an investigation of archival documents. He has revealed the specific features to no one yet, so that this will be news to all of us."

He sat down again, at the same time as Ranid stood up and began to speak.

"The facts that I have uncovered are startling and promise to overturn the idea systems of the older streams who long ago divided during the Great Schism. They promise to have extraordinary effects on the thinking of both currents within Amphibianism.

"I have stumbled upon a clear exposition of the conjoining, unifying viewpoint many generations ago, many years back in the past. In fact, at the climactic moment of the Great Schism itself.

"And who is the one who wrote such a prefigurement of our philosophy?

　　　CLEMENT S. MASLOFF

"No one else but Alsike Caldus himself."

A collective sigh of shock and surprise seemed to become audible to everyone present. All eyes focused on the speaker.

Ranid decided to plow ahead with a plan of action.

"At the convention about to begin at the Hypogeum, I intend to read the most central portions of this correspondence. For the ideas of the Institutor of Salamandrism were addressed to no one but the founder of Anuranism, Vahid Devre."

The sound from the audience rose to a soft murmuring.

"I sincerely believe that what I read out will echo far beyond the Hypogeum. The words put down so long ago by Alsike Caldus will affect the thinking of untold thousands." He looked about the salon, then went on. "We should immediately take advantage of this surprise by holding a spontaneous parade and demonstration about the center of Caecilia City. We should steer this march past both the Anuran and Salamandrine headquarters, so as to prove our strength in numbers and fervor. This will win for us the attention of the members of both of these spiritual strains."

A frenzy boiled up in the minds of his listeners.

Ranid foresaw strong, solid support from an enormous crowd of Conjoiners. That would provide a weapon of victory in the looming conflict ahead. It would overwhelm all its opponents.

Talem Devre walked a wild, random route through the dark streets of central Caecilia City that evening. His thoughts weighed on his brain like a pile of heavy slag.

There was a way out for the Anurans, he thought. But it necessitated a dangerous gamble. And he was the only person who could carry it out.

Did he have sufficient skill and courage to manage what had to be done?

Could he direct events in a desired direction?

Gritting his teeth, Talem decided to test his capability for action.

First of all, how was he to arrange a meeting with the Salamandrine Capitular, Caudo Eminius? That could not be done by merely announcing himself at the gate of the enemy's compound. Some convenient pretext had to be found to facilitate his approach.

Talem walked up to the front portal of the Citadelle, the huge castle of the Salamandrites. Agate, silica, flint, and rock crystals reflected the light from street lanterns. The great building resembled some magical castle out of the faraway past.

Taking a blank card and a stylo from his coat pocket, he wrote down a sentence and his name.

When he pressed a humming sounder, it brought an attendant to the gate.

The Anuran handed his message to the startled subordinate.

What would the reaction of the top official turn out to be? he asked himself as he waited. At last, the uniformed doorkeeper returned.

"Follow me, please," the man told Talem. "The Capitulary is descending because he wishes to see you."

It was evident that the plea had worked in drawing attention. "Must meet with you at once. I have the secret of how to defeat our common enemy. Signed Talem Devre, Head Secretary to the Anuran Syndics Board."

That had been enough to attract the interest of the top power-holder in the system of Salamandrism.

Talem followed the uniformed man down a long, narrow corridor.

"He will be with you shortly in there," said the attendant, pointing to a greenwood door. Opening it and cautiously entering, Devre found a dimly lit triangular cabinet with a cardwood table and two folding chairs. He sat down and awaited what was to come next.

The door opened and a ghostly shape clothed in solid black entered the strange room.

 CLEMENT S. MASLOFF

Talem recognized the Capitulary at once from photochrome pictures in the news journals. He started to rise, but the official gave a hand signal for him to remain seated.

"I am thoroughly amazed by your short note of introduction, sir," began Eximius, standing upright before the visiting Anuran. "My hope is that what you say on your card is true."

"I believe so with all my heart," declared the visitor. "What I wrote is not a lie. It can be substantiated. Everyone is going to believe what it says."

"Please explain what you mean, then."

"A person named Ranid Rolius, a Conjoiner, asked to study in the Devre family archive..."

The Capitulary interrupted him.

"Ranid Rolius! That name is familiar to me. I have collided with such an individual in the past. He was, at one time, a serious Salamandrine student with exceptional scholarly talents. But then we had to expel him from our organization for serious doctrinal irregularities and heretical ideas. But please go on with what you were saying."

Talem did just that, taking only a few minutes to describe the archival discovery that Ranid had made by himself.

Eximius grew ever redder in the face as he heard more and more.

At last, the narrative of the visitor came to an end and the official spoke again.

"He claimed to have done the same thing in our archives: discovered documents previously unknown because of incorrect labeling and cataloging."

Talem now bit his lower lip.

"He must not be permitted to create new libels based on false attributions and phony claims. I believe I know how to defeat what he plans to do at this convention of Conjoiners."

"What is that?" demanded Eximius with an anxious face.

"I have taken the letters that this man attributes to Alsike Caldus and have concealed them well. They are no longer in the Devre family archive. Thus, Rolius has no material platform to stand on, none whatsoever."

The Capitulary smiled sardonically.

"But what will happen tomorrow when these heretics meet?"

"The center of Caecilia City must be flooded with proclamations opposing his fraudulent claims. My own sister can be convinced to denounce him and swear that there never were such letters in our family's possession. They never existed at all, she will learn to say, backing me up. All of this will prove that Ranid Rolius is nothing more than a liar and imposter. His claims are pure fraud, nothing more than that."

Eximius, still standing, thought hard with a lot of exertion.

"You must compose such a broadside attack," he said. "Then, we will copy and print it for distribution. This is one time when we have to work together, despite our many differences. There is no alternative for either of us under present circumstances."

Dawn surged bright and clear over the Hypogeum, and the participants and audience were already arriving and being seated by specially assigned Conjoiners. The great throng entered the hall in solemn quiet, as if acknowledging the potential historical importance of this day and event.

Men and women displayed cards and badges and identities were verified.

No food or beverages were to be available for this serious, sober occasion.

The interior of the Hypogeum was lit by abundant gas lanterns high above the crowded floor.

Few conversations occurred among those being seated in the tiers of the hall.

On the raised rostrum, Dixo and Ereth went over the schedule for the day with Dr. Sugal. The morning would be taken up with necessary organizational business. Rules and structures were to result for the expanding movement. The main speeches were to be heard after a noon recess. All three leaders knew that address was to come from Ranid, who was not present at the moment. He was still back at the depot hotel, preparing and rehearsing the presentation of the spectacular revelations he was determined to make.

Meanwhile, something with consequences was happening at the Devre residence.

Talem rose and appeared downstairs early, as his sister was finishing her breakfast.

The brother sat down in the kitchen alcove, just as she was about to rise from the table.

"This is the day the heretics begin their convention sessions," said Talem, staring at his sister. "I have taken certain actions that will result in their collapse as an important movement."

Dera opened her mouth but said nothing.

"I have removed the letters sent to our ancestor," he went on. "There is no longer any proof of what this Ranid Rolius claims he will make public before the assembled Conjoiners. He can now be attacked as a fraudulent liar, a criminal faker. There is no way that the man can prove what he will say before his fanatics.

"And it has happened that I now have an important ally in erasing this radical danger.

"The Capitulary of the Salamandrites is going to coordinate an assault upon our common enemy. There is no way that the Conjoiners can survive as a credible stream of thought and belief when this opposition arises."

Dera looked confused and disturbed.

"Will any harm come to Ranid Rolius?" she bluntly asked him.

He replied with a hollow laugh. "Let me say this: I myself would not be connected to anything like that. You know me well enough to realize that, Dera."

She looked away from him. Neither one of them said anything more.

Talem finally excused himself and left the Devre residence.

Chapter XXXIV

At the appointed time that morning, Eleth moved onto the speaker's rostrum and began the official convention.

"Sisters and brothers. I herewith proclaim the founding congress of the Conjoining Association opened. Warm greetings to each and every one of you who have come to the Hypogeum.

"We know why we are here. What humans have dreamed of and striven for over many ages is now within grasp. The true, proper path to sanctification and enlightenment can be seen. It has become available to our generation.

"All of us have grown up as Amphibiots, of either the one variety or the other. We know their doctrines and principles, yet have long felt the inner spiritual emptiness of both of them. The deep morass of the rest of the population of Caecilia was also ours until we were awakened to a greater truth, a higher understanding. And now we have come together to express the message we have all received from the swamps of our country. We have conjoined ourselves into something greater.

"Our present task is clear. These teachings must be made available to all. We deserve the same rights and privileges as the older streams. Our duty today is to elevate ourselves through organization, mobilization, and aggressive recruitment. All of us know what we have to do.

"This morning the floor shall be opened for statements and proposals from our delegates. Then, this afternoon, several of our pioneers will come to the rostrum to present their ideas.

"Once again, I welcome all of you who are gathered here.

"Bless and keep you, dear brother and sisters.

"I hereby open the First Congress of the Conjoiners."

Loud cheering filled the Hypogeum to its highest rafter.

Ranid sat at his desk in his room of the depot hotel, going over the notes of his afternoon speech. He realized that what he planned to say would ignite an inextinguishable fire. At the center of the coming conflagration, he readied himself to reveal what Alsike Caldus was thinking when the Great Schism occurred.

How was he going to phrase his provocative revelation?

I cannot speak too fast or too harshly, he told himself. My goal must be to communicate a disturbing message while maintaining my emotional links with the audience.

Again he went through every point that he was to make that afternoon.

Meantime, preparations he knew nothing of were going on throughout the capital.

Capitular Caudo Eximius had had little sleep the prior night, directing the actions of the Salamandrites. He was going to prove that the Conjoiner claims concerning Alsike Caldus were lies. A river of pamphlets was to be released to overthrow the assertions of Ranid Rolius. The old, traditional faith was to be confirmed, with the Institutor at its center. The Conjoiners were to fall and fail.

Eximius was simultaneously confident and worried.

His plan appeared clear and clever, but it might fail without good luck.

Timing would surely be decisive in deciding the final outcome.

Only after Ranid made his claims public, was the counterforce against him to go into action. The war would then be on.

It was difficult to have to wait. There were spies in the Hypogeum who were to report when Rolius was finished making his surprise revelations.

CLEMENT S. MASLOFF

That was the moment he was to give the signal to release the pamphlets to the press and the public.

Eximius envisioned a renaissance of Salamandrism after the exposure of Ranid's falsehoods. That would be a sweet revenge on this renegade, he gloated.

But something of unnoticed importance was happening at that moment.

Dera Devre, in a cloak of red and green, was entering the central magneto-train depot and heading for the hotel that served as Conjoiner headquarters.

Once in the gigantic terminal, strangers directed her to the right location.

A Conjoiner told her which floor and room number to seek out.

"Thank you," she said as she went toward the levator that went up to where Ranid was.

The sound of the door zumbido interrupted the man working on his speech notes.

Ranid rose and went to see who it was. He was unprepared to see Dera standing there.

"Come in," he mumbled, then closed the door behind her.

"I have something of importance to tell you," she began. "My brother, whom you have never met, has committed a rotten act meant to harm you and your cause."

He asked her to take a chair while wondering if she were fantasizing some exaggerated drama.

"Talem, my baby brother, is head secretary to the syndics of the Anurans. He learned from what I told him about your research in our family archive. For reasons of his own, he looked at those letters and reached opposite conclusions. He decided to thwart any attempt by you to publicize your interpretation of the position of Alsike Caldus. He went to the Capitulary of the Salamandrites and gave him the letters, hoping to bring about an alliance of the two major movements against you and the Conjoiners.

"There is now a scheme to denounce and disprove your message as soon as you present it to the convention. This is aimed at leading to the swift disintegration of what you have started."

Ranid, still standing, drew heavy breaths of air. Only when his mind was back in equilibrium did he venture to speak again.

"I am deeply in your debt, my friend." He moved to his desk and picked up his notes, looking them over a moment.

"I shall have to revise my remarks to the convention," he said, nearly to himself.

Dera stared as the man she had tried to rescue threw the stack of cards into the trash barrel on the floor of the hotel room.

Ranid, resting a short time on the futon in the room, reviewed his history with both major poles of the Amphibiot faith.

All these years, I have restrained myself from aggressive steps, concealing what I know about the secret Apodists who run the Salamandrine faith. An inner sense of propriety inhibited me from making what I knew public. I hid what I had uncovered about that conspiracy in order to protect the reputation of Alsike Caldus as a great figure in Amphibiot history.

But today, with the Conjoiners close to victory, I shall be denounced as a liar and forger of letters. Shall an untrue libel be the weapon of our ruin? Are we to be the victims of trickery?

A new idea now rose in the mind of Ranid.

He was going to have to do what he had for years avoided, what he had considered impossible to carry out.

An invisible boundary had vanished and he had to place all the cards he held on the table now.

   CLEMENT S. MASLOFF

Ranid rode to the Hypogeum in a specially hired jitney. He asked Dera to accompany him. Both of them kept silent on their trip to the middle of Caecilia City.

Once they reached the subterrane convention hall, he took his companion with him through a back entrance, up to the raised platform where he was to give his address. "Take a chair up here," he told her. "You will be surprised at what I tell this audience."

The hall, filling up after the noon recess, was ready for the second session.

Eleth rose and began the proceedings. It took him only seconds to introduce the main speaker of the day, of the whole convention.

Thundering applause rang through the Hypogeum as Ranid rose from his chair and advanced to the podium.

When sufficient silence prevailed, he began in a powerful, ringing voice.

"Sisters and brothers in the faith, I am gratified to be present to talk to you on this historic occasion.

"We are here today to inaugurate a campaign to win the Amphibiots of Caecilia to the united, consolidated faith we hold to. Our train is on its way. No one can stop our progress. We are an army assured of our victory.

"But there are matters from the past that cannot be ignored, but must be faced. I myself have lived as a Salamandrite and as an Anuran, first the one and then the other. I received experience on how each stream functions. I possess a unique background that led me to Conjoinism as solution to the corruption and conflicts of the past.

"Yes, I speak of corruption that appalled me in earlier years of life.

"Let me tell you of a secret that is hidden at the core of Salamandrism, first of all.

"There is an unknown, invisible cabal that has from the foundation of that movement ruled its syndics from behind a curtain. No one sees or hears these phantom chieftains. They form an unseen circle whose teachings are an arcane form of Apodism."

Ranid proceeded to describe the secrets of the conspiracy he had uncovered years before and until that moment kept to himself.

He described the power that the Apod group exercised from its height.

The stunned audience listened as if turned to stone. A new, unfamiliar history of the Amphibiot multiple rainbow was heard for the first time. People heard a version of history totally unknown to them until now.

Chapter XXXV

Looking out at the nearly hypnotized faces, Ranid knew he had won them over to his viewpoint. No doubts would follow, no questioning of his leadership.

He turned around and walked back to take the chair beside Dera. She looked at him with a flood of tears in her eyes.

Dixo, Ereth, and Dr. Sugal stepped over to shake his hand.

Ranid suddenly remembered that he had not said a single word about the pre-Conjoiner ideas of Alsike Caldus. There was no reason for him to have done so, considering his stunning victory on another front. He could foresee that there would be no counterattack to possible revelations he had not made about the Devre correspondence of the great Institutor. His silence on that matter compelled equal reticence by those who had been ready to attack him through pamphlets. Their allegations were now made moot by his tactic of ignoring the subject of the letters in his shocking address to the Conjoiner convention.

He turned to Dera and whispered. "Let's return to the depot. That is where I will meet anyone who wishes to merge with us in a united movement."

On the jitney ride back to the depot hotel, Dera settled down and began to tell Ranid how she evaluated the situation.

"I think that I can do something for you and the Conjoiners. My brother still has the letters from Alsike in his possession. He gave the Capitular only copies. I plan to convince him to place the correspondence back in our family archive, where it belongs."

"Can you convince him to do that?" asked Ranid.

"I am certain I can," she replied with a hint of a smile.

The jitney rolled on to the magneto-train station, soon to become the national headquarters of the burgeoning, expanding movement.

⚊⚊

"What have you concluded from our most recent developments?" Ranid asked Hyle in the privacy of the latter's Archivum sanctum. It was several days after the triumphant convention ended.

The older man looked across his antique lancewood desk with a dreamy look.

"It is hard to say, my friend. "My mind has grasped for longer perspective as the years, then the decades, have passed. I have witnessed a lot. It is difficult to reach conclusions that are valid for too long. The turns of our history as a system of shared beliefs have been surprising and ever-changing. Only very little remains certain and credible. That is the unfortunate truth.

"But here is what I am sure of: there will be many changes that no one at present can predict or describe. They will come at us and our descendants out of the blue. No one is able to anticipate these developments. Some will be slow, others rapid and radical. But they will all be highly surprising to those who witness them.

"The Conjoiners may, for instance, in the future break up into separate schools of thought. What these will consist of and quarrel about, no one now knows. Vision ahead from today is impossible.

"Impossible?" asked Ranid with concern.

"Exactly like the splits and divisions in the past and in our own day," replied Hyle in a deeply solemn tone. "No one, least of all I, can define what those disagreements will be. They have not yet happened. No one can today say what their content will consist of. I even foresee a time when all the agents of the odyle are forgotten and allowed to vanish, leaving the universal odyle alone to focus upon."

     CLEMENT S. MASLOFF

All at once, Ranid gave a warm, happy grin. "It appears, then, that there will be a lot for everyone to look forward to, though in ignorance. Who can know what is coming in the days to come."

With that, he stood up, took his leave, and departed.